TIMBER LINE

MAX BRAND®

SAGEBRUSH
Large Print Westerns

First published in the United States by Five Star

First Isis Edition
published 2018
by arrangement with
Golden West Literary Agency

A catalogue record for this book is available
from the British Library.

ISBN 978–1–78541–556–2 (pb)

Published by
F. A. Thorpe (Publishing)
Anstey, Leicestershire

Set by Words & Graphics Ltd.
Anstey, Leicestershire
Printed and bound in Great Britain by
T. J. International Ltd., Padstow, Cornwall

This book is printed on acid-free paper

Table of Contents

ABOVE THE LAW

Appearing in the August 31, 1918 issue *of All-Story Weekly*, "Above the Law" was Frederick Faust's first published Western story. Although his editor Robert Davis had told him to emulate Zane Grey, with this first story Faust immediately displayed his own distinctive approach to Western fiction. While a sense of place other than the mythical West is absent, the unusual characters resonate in the reader's mind long after the story is read. "Above the Law" opens in a Western eatery where we are introduced to the fascinating heroine, La Belle Geraldine, Jerry — an actress and an outsider from the East, along with fellow actor, Freddie Montgomery, both slinging slang. Little do either realize the far-reaching impact the robber, Black Jim, will have on their lives when they decide to stage a robbery with Freddie posing as the infamous outlaw. The story was brought to the screen by Fox in 1918 as LAWLESS LOVE, starring Jewel Carmen and Henry Woodward.

CHAPTER
ONE

"Two Thousand Dollars Reward"

Her eyes were like the sky on a summer night, a color to be dreamed of but never reproduced. From the golden hair to the delicate hands which cupped her chin, a flower-like loveliness kept her aloof from her surroundings, like a rare pearl set in base metal. Her companion, young and darkly handsome, crumpled in a hand, scarcely less white than hers, the check which the waiter had left. In the meantime, he gazed with some concern at his companion. Her lips stirred. She sighed.

"Two dollars for ham and . . . in a jay dump," she murmured. "Can you beat it, Freddie?"

"He sort of sagged when we slipped him the order," answered the dark and distinguished youth. "I guess the hens are only making one-night stands in this country."

"They've got an audience, anyway," she returned, "and that's more than we could draw." She opened her purse and passed two bills to him under the table.

"Why the camouflage?" he asked, as he took the money.

"Freddie," she said, "run your glass eye over the men in this joint. If they see you pay for the eats with my money, they'd take you for a skirt in disguise." A light twinkled for an instant far back in her eyes.

"Take *me* for a skirt?" said Frederick Montgomery in his most austere manner. "Say, cutie, lay off on the rough stuff and get human."

Her lazy smile caressed him. "Freddie," she purred, "you do your dignity bit, the way Charlie Chaplin would do *Hamlet*"

Mr. Montgomery scowled upon her, but the dollar bills in the palm of his hand changed the trend of his thoughts at once. "Think of it, Jerry," he groaned, "if we hadn't listened to that piker Delaney, we'd be doing small . . . big time . . . over the R. and W.!"

"Take it easy, dearie," La Belle Geraldine answered. "I've still got a hundred iron men . . . but that isn't enough to take both of us to civilization."

Montgomery cleared his throat, frowned, and raised his head like a patriot making a death speech in the third act. "Geraldine," he said solemnly, "it ain't right for me to sponge on you. Now you take the money. It'll get you back to Broadway. As for me . . . I . . . I can go to work in one of the mines with these ruffians."

La Belle Geraldine chuckled. "You couldn't do it without a make-up, Freddie. And, besides, think of spoiling those hands with a pick-handle!"

Mr. Montgomery regarded his tender palms with a rather sad complacency. "There's no other way out, Jerry. Besides, I can . . . I can . . ." His voice trailed away drearily, and La Belle Geraldine regarded him with the familiar twinkle far back in her eyes.

"You're a born hero, Freddie . . . on the stage. But we're minus electric lights out here, and the play's no good."

4

"We're minus everything," declared Freddie with heat, overlooking the latter part of her speech. "This joint hasn't even got a newspaper in it, unless you call this rag one." He pulled out a crumpled paper, a single sheet printed raggedly on either side. Geraldine took it and regarded it with languid interest.

"The queer thing," she muttered, as she read, "is that I sort of like this rube gang out here, Freddie."

"Like them?" snorted her companion, as he shook down his cuffs and tightened his necktie. "Say, Jerry, you're talking in your sleep. Wake up and get next to yourself. Pipe the guy in the corner piling fried potatoes on his knife with a chunk of bread."

She turned her head. "Kind of neat action, all right," she said critically. "That takes real courage, Freddie. If his hand slipped, he'd cut his throat. Don't be so sore on them. As parlor snakes, they aren't in your class, but don't spend all your time looking at the stage set. Watch the show and forget the background, Freddie. These boys may eat with knives and get a little too familiar with their revolvers, but they strike me as being a hundred percent men."

"You always were a nut, Jerry," yawned Montgomery. "For my part, give me the still small voice, but not the wilderness. I can see all the rough nature I want in the Central Park Zoo." He pushed back his chair.

"Wait a minute, Freddie. Hold the curtain while I play the overture. I've got an idea. Listen to this." She spread out the Snider Gulch *Clarion* and read:

5

Attention, men of Snider Gulch, it's up to us! The citizens of Three Rivers have organized to rid the mountains of Black Jim. Prominent miners of that town have placed two thousand dollars on deposit, and offered it for the capture of the bandit, dead or alive. Men, is Snider Gulch going to be left behind by a jerk-water shanty village like Three Rivers? No! Let's get together. If Three Rivers can offer two thousand dollars for the capture of Black Jim, Snider Gulch can offer three thousand easy. We've got to show Three Rivers that we're on the map!

"How's that for a line of talk, Freddie?"

"What's the point?" he queried. "What do you get out of that monologue?"

"Wait a minute, the drums are still going out in the orchestra and your cue hasn't come yet. But before I get through, I'm going to ring up the curtain on a three-act melodrama that'll fill the house and give the box office insomnia."

She went on with the reading.

We can't expect to land Black Jim in a hurry. The reward money will probably get covered with cobwebs before it's claimed. The men who get it will have their hands full, that's certain. If they can even find his hiding place, they will be doing their share of work.

There are a number of theories about the way he works. Some people think that he lives either in Snider Gulch or Three Rivers, and does his hold-ups on the side. No man has ever seen his face because of the black mask he wears over his eyes. All we know is that his hair is black and that he always rides a roan horse. But that ought to be enough to identify him.

Some hold that he hides in some gulch with a lot of other outlaws. They don't think he leads a gang because he always works alone, but they believe that other gunmen have found his hiding place and are living near him. If that is the case, and Black Jim can be found in his home, we will clean out the bandits who have given our town a black name.

If Black Jim is caught, he will surely hang. He hasn't kitted anyone yet, but he's wounded nine or ten, and if he's ever pressed hard there's sure to be a lot of bloodshed. However, it's up to the brave men of Snider Gulch to take the chance. If they get him, they'll probably get the rest of the gunfighters who have been sticking up stages (which is Black Jim's specialty), and robbing and killing lone miners and prospectors, which is the long suit of the rest of the crowd.

In conclusion, all we have to say is that the men who get the money for Black Jim's capture will earn it, and our respect along with it.

She dropped the paper. "Now do you see, Freddie?"

"I'm no psychic wonder, Jerry," he answered with some irritation. "How can I tell what act you're thinking of? Wait a minute!" He gaped at her with sudden astonishment. "Say, Jerry," he growled, "have you got a hunch that *I'm* going to go out and catch this man-eating Black Jim?"

She broke into musical laughter. "Freddie," she said, when she could speak again. "I'd as soon send you to capture the bandit as I'd send a baby with a paper knife to capture a machine gun. No, dearie, I know you want to get out of here, but I don't want you to start East in a coffin. It costs too much."

"Slip it to me easy, Jerry," he said, "or I'll get peeved."

"Don't make me nervous," she mocked. "I don't ask you to do anything rough, except to put on clothes like the ones the guys around here are wearing . . . heavy boots, overalls, broad-brimmed hat, red bandanna around the neck."

He stared at her without comprehension. "Do you think they'll pay to see me in an outfit like that?"

"They ought to, and it's my idea to make them. It's a nice little bit for us both, Freddie. First act starts like this. Stage set . . . a western mining town, Three Rivers. Enter the lead . . . a girl, stunning blonde, wears corduroy, walking skirt."

Montgomery grinned but still looked baffled. "You hate yourself all right," he said, "but lead on the action."

"Nobody knows why the girl is there, and nobody cares, because they don't ask questions in a mining town."

"Not even about the theater," groaned Montgomery.

"Shut up, Freddie," cut in La Belle Geraldine. "You spoil the scene with your monologue stunts. I say, the swell blonde appears and buys a seat on the stage that starts that afternoon, running toward Truckee. She kids the driver along a little, and he lets her sit on the seat beside him. As soon as she gets planted there, she begins to talk . . . let me see . . . yes, she begins to hand out a swift line of chatter about what she can do with a revolver. Then she shows him a little nickel-plated revolver that she carries with her. He asks her to show off her skill, but she says . . . 'Nothing stirring, Oscar.' Finally they go around a curve, and out rides a masked bandit on a roan horse. Everybody on the stage holds up their arms as soon as he comes out with his gun leveled."

"How do you know they would?" said Montgomery.

"Because they always do," answered Geraldine. "Nobody thinks of making a fight when a masked man on a roan horse appears, because they know it's Black Jim, who can shoot the core out of an apple at five hundred yards, or something like that. Well, they all hold up their hands except the girl, who raises her revolver and fires, and, although she used a blank cartridge, the gun jumps out of the grip of the bandit as if a bullet hit it. Then he holds up his hands, and everybody on the stage cheers, and the girl takes the bandit prisoner. The stage turns around and carries them back to Three Rivers. The people of the town come to look at Black Jim . . ."

"And they see I'm not the guy they want. Then the game's blown."

"Not a hope," said Jerry. "They don't know anything about this man-killer, except the color of his horse. They'll take you for granted."

"Sure," groaned Montgomery, "and hang me to the nearest tree, what?"

"Take it easy, Freddie. There's some law around here. You just keep your face shut after they take you. They'll wait to try you the next day, anyway. That'll give me time to cash in the reward. I'll be fifty miles past before they get wise. The next morning, when they come in to stick a rope on your neck, you simply light a cigarette and tell them it's all a mistake. Let 'em go to Snider Gulch, to the hotel, and they can find a hundred people to recognize you as a ham actor. Tell them you were merely trying a little act of your own, when you stuck up the stage, and that your partner flashed the gun from the driver's seat. Say, kid, the people of Three Rivers will see the laugh is on them, and they'll buy you a ticket to Denver just to get rid of you. I'll meet you there, and then we'll trot on to Broadway, savvy? It's a dream!"

"A nightmare," growled Montgomery, although light entered his face. "But still . . ."

"Well?"

"Jerry, I begin to think it wouldn't be such a hard thing to get away with this. But what if you couldn't get me out of the town? What if they started to lynch me without waiting for the law?"

"That's easy," smiled Geraldine. "Then I step out and tell them it's simply one grand joke. All we would have to be sorry about is the money we spent on your horse and clothes and gun. It's a chance, Freddie, but it's a chance that's worth taking. Two thousand dollars reward!"

10

Montgomery's eyes hardened. "Jerry," he whispered, "every stage that leaves Three Rivers has a lot of pure gold in the boot. Why not play the bandit part legitimate and grab the gold? It's a lot simpler, and there's no more risk."

Geraldine studied him curiously. "You've got the makings of a fine crook, Freddie. It's in your eye now."

He colored and glanced away.

"It's no go, dearie. If we cheat these miners with my little game, at least we know that the money comes only from the rich birds who can afford to put up a reward. But if we grab the cash in the boot, how can we tell we aren't taking the bread and jam out of the mouth of some pick swinger with a family to support?" She finished with a smile, but there was a suggestion of hardness in her voice.

"Jerry," he answered, "you're certainly fast in the bean. I'd go a ten-spot to a Canadian dime that you could make up with one hand and darn stockings with the other. We'll do it your way, if you insist. It'll be a great show."

"Right you are, Freddie. You've got the face for the act."

They had to spread a hundred dollars over a horse, a revolver, and Montgomery's clothes. He spent most of the day shopping and at night came home with the necessary roan, a tall animal which was cheapened by bad ring-bones. His clothes, except the hat and boots, were very inexpensive, and he managed to buy a second-hand revolver for six dollars.

While he made these purchases, La Belle Geraldine, now registered at the hotel under her real name as Annie Kerrigan, opened a conversation with the girl who worked in the store. She proved diffident at first, with an envious eye upon Jerry's hat with its jaunty feather curled along the side, but in the end La Belle's smile thawed the cold.

"She handed me the frosty eye," reported Jerry to Montgomery that evening, "until I put her wise on some millinery stunts. After that it was easy. She told me all she knew about Black Jim, and a lot more. People say he's a big chap . . . so are you, Freddie. His complexion is dark . . . so is yours. One queer thing is that he has never killed anyone. The paper said that, and the girl said it, too. It seems he's a big-time guy with a gun, and, when he shoots, he can pick a man in the arm or the leg, just as he pleases. I don't suppose you can hit a house at ten yards, Freddie, but it's a cinch they aren't going to try you out with a revolver . . . not as long as they have a hunch you're Black Jim."

That night Montgomery learned all that could be told about the stage route and the time it left Three Rivers. By dawn of the next day he and Jerry were on the road toward Three Rivers by different routes.

CHAPTER
TWO

'Hands Up!'

The happiness of women, say the moralists, depends upon their ability to preserve illusions. Annie Kerrigan punched so many holes in that rule that she made it look like a colander. Illusions and gloom filled her earlier girlhood in her little Illinois home town. Those illusions chiefly concerned men. They made the masculine sex appear vast in strength and illimitable in mystery.

She remembered saying to a youth who wore a white flower in his lapel and parted his hair in the middle and curled it on the sides: "When I talk to you, I feel as if I were poking at a man in armor. I never find the *real* you. What is it?"

The youth occupied two hours in telling her about the "real you." He was so excited that he held her hand as he proceeded in the revelation. When he left, she boiled down everything he had said. It was chiefly air, and all that wasn't air was surrounded with question marks so large that even Annie Kerrigan could see them. So she revised her opinion of men a little.

In place of part of the question marks she substituted quotations. As she grew older and prettier, she learned more. In fact, she learned a good deal more than she wished to know about every attractive youth in her town. So Annie Kerrigan started out to conquer new worlds of knowledge.

Her family balked, but Annie was firm. She went to Chicago, where she found the stockyards — and more men. They smiled at her in the streets. They stared at her in restaurants. They accosted her at corners. So the mystery wore off.

About this time Annie was left alone in the world to support herself. She starved for six months in a department store. Then an enterprising theatrical manager offered her a chance in a third-rate vaudeville circuit.

Before that season ended, she had completed her definition of men. In her eyes they were one-half quotation marks and the other half bluff. Every one of them had his pet mystery and secret. Annie Kerrigan found that, if she could get them to tell her that secret, they forged their own chains of slavery and gave her the key to the lock.

In time she held enough keys to open the doors of a whole city full of masculine souls. But she never used those keys, because, as she often said to herself, she wasn't interested in interior decoration. The exceptions were when she wanted a raise in salary or a pleasure excursion.

In this manner Annie Kerrigan of many illusions and more woes developed into La Belle Geraldine with no illusions: a light heart and a conscience that defied insomnia. She loved no one in particular — not even

14

herself — but she found the world a tolerably comfortable place. To be sure, it was not a dream world. La Belle Geraldine was so practical that she knew cigarettes stain the fingers yellow and increase the pulse. She even learned that Orange Pekoe tea is pleasanter than cocktails, and that men are more often foolish than villainous.

Without illusions, the mental courage of Jerry equaled that of a man. Therefore, she commenced this adventure without fear or doubt of the result. It was a long journey, but her lithe, strong body, never weakened by excess, never grown heavy with idleness, shook off the fatigue of the labor, as a coyote that has traveled all day, and all night shakes off its weariness and trots on, pointing its keen nose against the wind. So she went on, sometimes humming an air, sometimes pausing an instant to look across the valley at the burly peaks — and far beyond these, range after range of purple-clad monsters, like a great hierarchy whose heads rise closer and closer to heaven itself. She found herself smiling and for no cause whatever.

She had estimated the distance to Three Rivers at about ten miles. Yet it seemed to her that she had covered scarcely a third of that space, when the road twisted down and she was in the village. It was even smaller than Snider Gulch. The type of men to which she had grown accustomed during the past few weeks swarmed the street. They paid little attention to her, even as she had expected. Mountains discourage personal curiosity.

The six horses were already hitched to the stage, and baggage was piled in the boot. After she bought a passage to Truckee, her money was exhausted. If she failed, the prospect was black, indeed. She could not even telegraph for help, particularly since there was not a telegraph line within two days' journey. She shrugged this thought away as unworthy.

When the passengers climbed up to select their seats, Geraldine remained on the ground to talk with the driver about his near leader, a long-barreled bay with a ragged mane and a wicked eye. The driver as he went from horse to horse, examining tugs and other vital parts of the harness, informed her that the bay was the best mountain horse he had ever driven, and that with this team he could make two hours' better time than on any of the other relays between Three Rivers and Truckee.

She showed such smiling interest in this explanation that he asked her to sit up on his seat, while he detailed the other points of interest about this team. Her heart quickened. The first point in the game was won. As they swung out onto the shadowed road — for the cañons were already half dark, although it was barely sunset — she made a careful inventory of the passengers. There were nine besides herself, and all were men. Two of them, sitting just behind the driver, held sawed-off shotguns across their knees and stared with frowning sagacity into the trees on either side of the road, as if they already feared an attack. Their tense expectancy satisfied La Belle Geraldine that the first appearance of her bandit would take the fight out of them. The others were mostly young fellows who hailed each other in loud voices and broke into an immediate exchange of mining gossip. She feared nothing from any of these.

The driver worried her more. To be sure, his only weapon was a rifle which lay along the seat just behind him, with its muzzle pointing out to the side, a clumsy position for rapid work. But his lean face with the small, sad eyes made her guess at qualities of quiet fearlessness. However, it was useless to speculate on the chances for or against the masked and waiting Montgomery. The event could not be more than half an hour away.

They had scarcely left Three Rivers behind, when she produced the small revolver from her pocket. The driver grinned and asked if it were loaded. It was a sufficient opening for Geraldine. She sketched briefly for his benefit a life in the wilds during which she had been brought up with a rifle in one hand and a revolver in the other. The stage driver heard her with grim amusement, while she detailed her skill in knocking squirrels out of a tree top.

"The top of a tree like that one, lady?" he asked, pointing out a great sugar pine.

"You don't believe me?" asked Jerry with a convincing assumption of pique. "I wish there was a chance for me to show you."

"Hmm!" said the driver. "There's a tolerable lot of things for you to aim at along the road. Take a whirl at anything you want to. The horses won't bolt, when they hear the gun."

"If I did hit it," said Jerry with truly feminine logic, "you would think it was luck." She dropped the pistol back into the pocket of her dress. They were swinging around a curve that brought them to the foot of the long slope, at the top of which Montgomery must be waiting.

"I hope something happens," she assured the driver, "and then I'll show you real shooting."

"Maybe," he nodded, "I've lived so long, nothin' surprises me, lady."

She smiled into the fast-growing night and made no answer. Then she broke out into idle chatter again, asking the names of all the horses and a thousand other questions, for a childish fear came to her that he might hear the beating of her heart and learn its meaning. Up they drudged on the long slope, the harness creaking rhythmically as the horses leaned into the collars, and the traces stiff and quivering with the violence of the pull. The driver with his reins gathered in one hand and the long whip poised in the other, flicked the laggards with the lash.

"Look at them lug all together as if they was tryin' to keep time!" he said to Geraldine. "I call that a team, but this grade here keeps them winded for a half an hour after we hit the top."

The rank odor of the sweating horses rose to her. A silence, as if their imaginations labored with the team, fell upon the passengers. Even Geraldine found herself leaning forward in the seat, as though this would lessen the load.

"Yo-ho, boys!" shouted the driver. "Get into that collar, Dixie, you wall-eyed excuse for a hoss! Yea, Queen, good girl!" His whip snapped and hummed through the air. "One more lug altogether and we're there!"

They lurched up onto the level ground, and the horses, still leaning forward to the strain of the pull, stumbled into a feeble trot. Jerry sat a little sidewise in the seat so that from the corner of her eye she could watch the rest of the passengers. One of the guards was lighting a cigarette for the other.

"Hands up!" called a voice.

The driver cursed softly, and his arms went slowly into the air; the hands of the two guards shot up even more rapidly. Not three yards from the halted leaders, a masked man sat on a roan horse, reined across the road, and covered the stage with his revolver.

"Keep those hands up!" ordered the bandit. "Now get out of that stage . . . and don't let your hands down while you're doin' it! You-all, there by the driver, get up your hands damned quick!"

CHAPTER
THREE

"The Mixed Cast"

A great tide of mirth swelled in Jerry's throat. She recognized in these deep and ringing tones, the stage voice of Freddie Montgomery. Truly he played his part well.

She crouched a little toward the stage driver, whipped out the revolver, and fired — but a louder explosion blended with the very sound of her shot. The revolver spun out of her fingers and exquisite pain burned her hand.

Her rage kept her from screaming. She groaned between her set teeth. This was an ill day for Frederick Montgomery!

"For God's sake!" breathed a voice from the stage behind her. "He'll kill us all now! It's Black Jim!"

"Down to the road with you," cried the bandit, in the same deep voice, "and the next of you-all that tries a fancy trick, I'll drill you clean!"

Warm blood poured out over her hands and the pain set her shuddering, but the white hot fury gave her strength. Jerry was the first to touch the ground.

"You fool!" she moaned. "You big, clumsy, square-headed, bat-eyed, fool! They'll stick you in the pen for life for this!"

"Shut up!" advised a cautious voice from the stage, where the passengers stood bolt upright, willing enough to descend, but each afraid to move. "Shut up or you'll have him murdering us all!"

"Sorry, lady," said the masked man, and still he maintained that heavy voice. "If I had seen you was a girl, I wouldn't have fired!"

"Aw, tell that to the judge," cried Geraldine. "You've shot my hand off! I'll bleed to death, and you'll hang for it! I tell you, you'll hang for it!"

He had reined his horse from his position in front of the leaders, and now he swung from his saddle to the ground, a sudden motion during which he kept his revolver steadily leveled.

"Easy in there," he ordered, "and get the hell out of that stage, or I'll blow you out!" He gestured with his free hand to Jerry. "Tear off a strip from your skirt and tie that hand up as tight as you can. Here, one of you, get down here and help the lady. You can take your hands down to do that."

But there was another thought than that of La Belle Geraldine in the mind of the practical stage driver. His leaders stood now without obstruction. He had lost one passenger, indeed, but the gold in the boot of his stage was worth a hundred passengers to him. He shouted a warning, dropped flat on his seat, and darted his whip out over the horses. At his call the other passengers groveled flat, which put the thickness of the boot between them and the bullets of the bandit. The horses hit the collars, and the stage whirled into the dusk of the evening.

To pursue was folly, for it would be a running fight with two deadly shotguns handled by men concealed and protected. The masked man fired a shot over the heads of the fugitives and turned on Jerry. She was weak with excitement and loss of blood and even her furious anger could not give her strength for long. She staggered.

"I'm done for, all right," she gasped. "As a bandit, you're the biggest cheese ever. My hand . . . blood . . . help . . ."

Red night swam before Jerry's eyes, and, as utter dark came, she felt an arm pass round her. When she woke from the swoon, her entire right arm ached grimly. She was being carried on horseback up a steep mountain side. The trees rose sheer above her. She strove to speak, but the intolerable weakness flooded back on her, and she fainted again.

She recovered once more in less pain, lying in a low-roofed room, propped up on blankets. A lantern hung against the wall from a nail, and, by its light, she made out the form of the man who stooped over her and poured steaming hot water over her hand. He still wore the mask. She closed her eyes again and lay gathering her wrath, her energy, and her vocabulary, for the supreme effort which confronted her.

"So you did your little bandit bit, did you?" she said at last with keen irony, as she opened her eyes again. "You had to pull the grandstand stunt with a fine audience often to watch you? You had to . . ."

"Lie still, don't talk," he commanded, still in that deep and melodramatic bass that enraged her. "You have a fever, kind of. It ain't much. Just keep quiet an' you'll be all right."

It was the crowning touch. He was still playing his part! "Dearie," she said fiercely, "this is the first time in my life I ever wished I was Shakespeare. Nobody, but the old boy himself, could do you justice . . . but I'm not Billy S., and I can only hint around sort of vague at what I think of you. But of all the tin-horn sports, the ham-fat, small-time actors, you're the prize bonehead. Honey, does that begin to percolate? Does that begin to get through the armor plate down to that dwarfed bean you're in the habit of calling your brain?"

He went on calmly, pouring the hot water over her hand. She had not credited him with such self-control. He did not even blush as far as she could make out. It made her throat dry with impotence.

"An old woman's home, that's where you belong," she went on. "Say, you're wise to keep that mask on. You'd need a disguise to get by as a property man on small time. Dearie, you haven't got enough bean to be number two man in a monologue."

He stared at her a moment and then went on with the work of cleansing the bullet wound in her hand. Evidently he did not trust himself to speak. It was not a severe cut, but it had bled freely, the bullet cutting the fleshy part between the thumb and forefinger. To look at it made her head reel. She lay back on the pile of blankets and closed her eyes.

When she opened them again, he was approaching with a small bottle half full of a brownish-black fluid, iodine. She started, for she knew the burn of the antiseptic. She tucked her wounded hand under her other arm and glared at him.

"Nothing doing with that stuff, cutie," she said, shaking her head. "This isn't my first season, even if I'm not on the big time. You can give that bottle to the Marines. Go pour that on the daisies, Alexander W. Flathead, it'll kill the insects. But not for mine."

She saw his forehead pucker into a frown above the mask. He stopped, hesitated,

"Take it away and rock it to sleep, Oscar," she went on, "because there's no cue for that in this act. It won't get across . . . not even with a make-up. Oh, this will make a lovely story when I get back to Broadway. I'm going to spill the beans, dearie. Yep, I'm going to give this spiel to the papers. It'll make a great ad for you . . . all scare heads. You can run the last musical comedy scandal onto the back page with a play like this. Here! Let go my arm, you big simp . . . do you think . . ."

He caught her wrist and drew out the injured hand firmly. She struggled weakly, but the pain in the hand unnerved her.

"Go ahead . . . turn on the fireworks, Napoleon! Honey, they'll write this on your tombstone for an epitaph."

He spread her thumb and forefinger apart, poured some of the iodine onto a clean rag, and swabbed out the wound. The burning pain brought her close to a faint, but her fury kept her mind from oblivion. She clenched her teeth so that a tortured scream became merely a moan. When she recovered, he was making the

24

last turn of a rather skillful bandage. She sat up on the blankets.

"All right, honey, now you've played the music, and I'll dance. What's the way to town from here?"

He shook his head.

"Won't tell me, eh? I suppose you think I'll stay up here till I get well? Think again, janitor." She rose and started a bit unsteadily toward the door. Before she reached it, his step caught up with her. She was swung up in strong arms and carried back to the blankets. While she sat dumb with hate and rage, he took a piece of rope and tied her ankles fast with an intricate knot that she could never hope to untie with her one sound hand.

"You'll stay here," he explained curtly.

"Listen, dearie," she answered between her teeth, "I'm going to do you for this. I'm going to make you a bum draw on every circuit in the little old U.S. I'm going to make you the card that doesn't fill the straight, that's all. Get your shingle ready, cutie, because, after this, all you can get across will be a chop-house in the Bowery."

"Lie still," growled the deep voice. "There ain't any chance of you getting away. Savvy?" He turned.

"Dearie," she cried after him, "if you don't cut out that ghost voice stunt, I'll . . ."

The rickety door at the back of the shack closed upon him.

"I never knew," said Jerry to herself, "that big Swede could do such a swell mystery bit. He ought to be in the heavies, that's all."

She settled herself back on the blankets again more comfortably. The last sting of the iodine died away and left a pleasant sense of warmth in her injured hand. Now she set about surveying her surroundings in detail. It was the most clumsily built house she had ever seen, made of rudely trimmed logs so loosely set together that the night air whistled through a thousand chinks.

Two boards placed upon sawhorses represented a table. A crazily constructed fireplace of large dimensions was the only means of heating the shack. Here and there, from pegs and nails driven into the wall, hung overalls, deeply wrinkled at the knees, heavy mackintoshes, and two large hats of broad brim. On the floor were several pairs of heavy shoes in various states of dilapidation. In the corner next to the hearth the walls were garnished with a few pots and pans. On the table she saw a heavy hunting knife.

There were three doors. Perhaps one of them led to a second room. To know which one was of vital significance to her. If it was the door through which the masked man had disappeared, then he was still within hearing distance. If that were true, she could hardly succeed in reaching that knife upon the table unheard, for she would make a good deal of noise dragging herself across the floor to the table. She determined to make the experiment. If she could cut the bonds and escape, she had no doubt that she could find the road to Three Rivers again, and even to wander across the mountains at night with a wounded hand was better than to stay with this bungler. Moreover, there was something in his sustained acting which made her uneasy. She knew his code of morals was as limited as the law of the Medes and the Persians and of an exactly opposite nature. On the stage, in the city, she had no fear of him. He was an interesting type, and his vices were things at which she could afford to shrug her shoulders. But in the wilderness of the silent mountains even the least of men borrows a significance, and the meaning he gave her was wholly evil.

She commenced hunching herself slowly and painfully across the floor toward the table. Half, three-quarters of the distance was covered. In another moment she could reach out and take the knife.

A door creaked behind her. She turned. There he stood again, still masked and with his hands behind him. He started. His mouth gaped. She made another effort and caught up the knife. At least it was a measure of defense, even if it were too late for her to free herself.

CHAPTER
FOUR

"Black Jim"

"Jerry!" he said, in a strange, whispering voice.

She eyed him with infinite disgust. "Playing a new role, Freddie, aren't you?" she sneered.

He merely stared.

"You're versatile, all right," she went on. "First the grim bandit, and then the astonished friend. Say, dearie, do you expect warm applause? No, cutie, but if I had some spoiled eggs, I'd certainly pass them to you."

"Jerry, you're raving!"

She gritted her teeth. "I'm through with the funny stuff, you one-syllable, lock-jawed baby. Now I mean business. Get me out of this as fast as they hooked you off the boards, the last time you tried out in Manhattan."

"Do you . . . have . . . will . . ."

"Bah!" she said. "Don't you get that I'm through with this one-night stand? Drop the curtain and start the orchestra on 'Home, Sweet Home.' Talk sense. Cut this rope. I'm starting, and I'm starting alone."

"For God's sake, Jerry."

"Lay off on that stuff, dearie. If words made a cradle, you'd rock the world to sleep."

"How . . . how did you come here?"

She stared at him a moment and then broke into rather sinister laughter.

"I suppose you've been walking in your sleep, what? I suppose I'm to fall for this bum line, Freddie? Not me! You can't get by even in a mask, Mister Montgomery."

"Geraldine."

"Can the talk, cutie. You can tell the rest to the judge."

"But how can I help you?" he asked. He turned, and she saw his hands tied securely together behind him!

While she still stared at this marvelous revelation, the door opened again and another Montgomery strode into the room. He was the same build as the other man. He wore the same sort of mask. His hair was black. He could not be Montgomery. It was only when they stood together that she felt a significant difference in this man. Seeing Jerry with the hunting knife in her hand, he crossed the room and leaned above her.

"Give me the knife!" boomed the musical bass voice.

She shrank back and clutched the heavy handle more closely. "Keep away," she cried hoarsely.

"Give me the knife."

"Black Jim!" breathed Jerry, for the first time wholly frightened, while her mind whirled in confusion. "Is the whole world made up of doubles, or am I losing my brain? Keep off, Mister Mystery, or I'll make hash of you with this cleaver!"

She held the knife poised, and the man observed her with a critical eye.

"Fighter," he decided.

He leaned forward, and his hand darted out with the speed of a striking snake. She cut at him furiously, but the hand caught her wrist and stopped the knife while it was still an inch from his face. He shook her hand, and the numbing grasp made her fingers relax. The knife clattered on the floor, and he carried her back to the pile of blankets. When she opened her eyes, she saw Black Jim loosing the hands of Montgomery.

"No use in we-all stayin' masked any more," said the bandit. "I've been down an' seen the other boys. I thought maybe they'd vote yes on turnin' the girl loose again. I told 'em she was too sick to see anything, when I brought her in. I told 'em I'd blindfold her, when I took her out to the road again. But they all sort of figure she'd be able to track back with a posse, followin' jest a sense of direction like a hoss. They vote that she stays here, an' so it makes no difference what she sees."

He finished untying Montgomery's hands, and drew off his mask.

Her faintness left Jerry. She saw a lean-faced man with great, dark eyes, singularly lacking in emotion, and forehead unfurrowed by worries. Montgomery likewise withdrew his mask and showed a face familiar enough, but drawn and colorless.

"All I'm askin'," said Black Jim, "is have you got anything against me?"

"I?" queried Montgomery, and he drew a slow hand across his forehead as if he were partially dazed.

"Yes, you," said the other, and the dark eyes dwelt carefully on Montgomery's face. "If you've got any lingerin' suspicion that there's something coming from

30

you to me, we'll jist nacherally step out an' make our little play where there's room."

"Not a thing against you, my friend," said Montgomery with a sudden heartiness for which Jerry despised him. "You had the drop on me, and I guess you had special reasons for wanting that stage."

The outlaw shrugged his shoulders. "I got to go out again," he said, "an' I'm goin' to ask you to watch this girl while I'm gone."

"Glad to," said Montgomery.

Black Jim turned, paused, and came back. "If anything happens to her, my friend." He hesitated significantly. "The boys seemed to be sort of excited, when I told them about her bein' in my cabin," he explained. "If they all come up here, don't let 'em come in. You got a gun!"

He stepped to the door and was gone. The eyes of Jerry and Montgomery met.

"Quick!" she ordered. "Talk out and tell me what has happened, Freddie, or I'll go crazy. I'm half out of my head now!"

"It's Black Jim!" he said heavily.

"I knew that half an hour ago. Your brains are petrified, Freddie. Start where I'm a blank. How'd you come here?"

"He held me up."

"Black Jim?"

"Yes. I was waiting behind the rock with my mask on. I heard a horse coming up the road from behind, and, when I turned, I was looking into the mouth of a pistol as big as a cannon. I put up my hands. I just

31

stared at him. I couldn't speak. He said he was sorry he couldn't leave the job to me. He said there were two things clear to him. He went on thinking them over while his gun covered me. Then he told me that he couldn't leave me alive near the road. He had to take me up to his camp. Then he came up behind me and tied my hands behind my back. Jerry, I felt that if he hadn't thought me one of his own sort, he'd have dropped the curtain on my act forever." He shuddered slightly at the thought.

"He made me ride before him up here," he went on, "and he put me in this cabin. As far as I can make out, we're in a little gulch of the mountains. It's a sort of a bandits' refuge. When we rode over the edge of the hill and dipped down into the valley, I saw some streaks of smoke down the cañon. There must be a half dozen places like this one, and some of the outlaws in every one. What'll we do, Jerry, for God's sake, what will we do?"

"Shut up!" she said fiercely, and her face was whiter than mere exhaustion could make it. "Lemme think, just lemme think!"

Montgomery had no eye for her. He strode up and down the room with a wild expression. He seemed to think of her as an aftermath.

"What happened to you? Was it Black Jim again?"

"I pulled my gun and shot in the air. He shot the pistol out of my fingers and put my hand on the blink. I fainted. He brought me up here. That's all." Her thoughts were not for her troubles.

32

"I'm going to make a break for it!" he cried at last. "Maybe I can get free."

"And leave me here?" she asked.

He flushed, stammered, and avoided her eyes. "It doesn't make any difference," he muttered. "I couldn't find my way out, and maybe they'd take a pot shot at me as I tried to get away. It's better to die quick than starve in the mountains. But, my God, Jerry, what'll he do, when he finds out that I'm not an outlaw like himself?"

"Stop crying like a baby," she said. "I've got to think." There's only one thing for you to do," she said at last, raising her head, "and that's for you to play your part as he sees it. You can act rough. Go down and mix with them . . . but be here with me when Black Jim is here. They can only kill you, Freddie, but me . . ." Her eyes were roving again.

"Maybe I can do it," he said rapidly, half to himself. "Pray God I can do it!"

CHAPTER
FIVE

"The Stage Man"

Her upper lip curled. "You're in a blue funk . . . a blue funk," she said. "Freddie, here's your one chance in a lifetime to play the man. Do you see *my* condition? Do you see the little act that's mapped out ahead for me? It's as clear as the palm of your hand. He brought me up here because he thought I'd die if he left me in the road. Even his heart was not black enough for that. But once he had me here, it wasn't in his power to send me away again. That's what he meant when he said he had talked to the boys. They wouldn't let me go because they thought I might be able to find the way back and bring a posse after them. Don't you see? They have me a prisoner. And you're all that I have to protect me." She stopped and moaned softly. "Why was I ever born a woman?"

He moistened his lips. "I'll do what I can," he mumbled, "but . . . did you see that devil's eye? He isn't human, Jerry."

I might have known, she murmured to herself, *I might have known he was only a stage man.* She said aloud: "There's one chance in a thousand left to me,

Freddie, but there's no chance at all, unless you'll help me. Will you?"

"All that I can ... in reason," he stammered miserably.

"It's this," she went on, trying to sweep him along with her. "You had your eyes open when you came up here. Maybe you could find the way out again. Freddie, you said on the road today that you loved me. Freddie, I'll go to hell and slave for you as long as I live, if you'll fight for me now. Tell me again that you love me and you'll be a man!"

His lips were so stiff he could hardly speak in answer. "I didn't tell you one thing," he said. "When we came over the top of the hill, at the edge of the valley, we passed an armed man. They keep a sentry there."

She pointed with frantic eagerness. "You have your gun at your belt. That will free us, I tell you. It is only one man you have to fight."

He could not answer. His eyes wandered rapidly around the room like a boy already late for school and striving miserably to find his necessary book.

"Then if you won't do that, cut the rope that holds my feet and I'll go myself!" she cried. "I'll go. I'd rather a thousand times die of starvation than wait for the time when the eyes of that fiend light up with hellfire."

"Black Jim," he answered, and stopped.

She loosened her dress at the throat, as if she stifled. "For God's sake, Freddie. You have a sister. I've seen her picture. For her sake!"

He was utterly white and striving to speak. "He would know it was me who did it," he said at last, "and then . . ."

Voices sounded far away. They listened with great eyes that stared at each other but saw only their own imaginings. The voices drew closer.

"The door . . . the door," she whispered. "Lock the door. They're coming . . . the men he warned us about."

He was frozen to the spot on which he stood.

"Hello!" called a voice from without.

"Montgomery," she moaned, wringing her hands.

At last he walked hastily to the door. "You can't come in here," he answered.

"Why the hell not?" roared one of them.

"Because of Black Jim."

A silence followed.

"Is he in there?"

"No, but he wants no one else to come in while he's gone."

They parleyed.

"Shall we chance it?" "Not me!" "Why not?" "Let's see his woman." "Sure. Seein' her doesn't do no harm." "Who's in there?" "It's the pal he brought up." "Are we goin' to act like a bunch of shorthorns?" asked a deeper voice. "I'm goin' in!"

A dozen men broke into the room. At the first stir of the door Jerry dropped prone to the blankets and feigned sleep. The crowd gathered first about Montgomery, searching him with curious eyes.

"Here's the new lamb," said a lithe, white-faced man, and he grinned over yellow teeth. "Here's another roped for the brandin'. Let's pass on him now, boys."

A chuckle, that rang heavily on the heart of Montgomery, ran around the circle, but, although his soul was lead in him, his art came to his rescue. After all, this was merely a part to be played. It was a dangerous part, indeed, but with a little effort he should be able to pass before an uncritical audience. He leaned back against the wall and smiled at the group. It required every ounce of his courage to manage that smile.

"Look me over, boys," he responded, "take a good long look, and in case you're curious, maybe you'll find something interesting on my right hip." He broke off the smile again. For one instant the scales hung in the balance. What he said might have been construed as a threat, but the smile took the sting out of his words. After all, a man who had been passed by Black Jim himself had some rights among them.

"You're a cool one, all right" — grinned a man who was bearded like a Russian, with his shirt open, and a great black, hairy chest partially exposed — "but where'd you get that color? Been doing inside work?"

"Mac's the name," said Montgomery easily, for the last remark gave him courage, "and some of the boys call me Silent Mac. I'm a bit off color, all right. That's because some legal gents got interested in me. They got so damned interested in me they thought I shouldn't be out in the sun so much. They thought maybe it was spoiling my complexion, see? They fixed a plant and

37

sent me up the river to a little joint the government runs for restless people. Yep, I've just had a long rest cure, and now I'm ready for business."

A low laugh of understanding ran around the group. A jailbird has standing in the shadow of the law.

"You'll do, pal," said the yellow-toothed one.

"You can enter the baby show, all right," said another. "I'm the Doctor."

"I've heard of you," said Montgomery, as the crowd passed him to examine Jerry.

"Know anything about the calico?" one asked Montgomery.

"Not a thing," answered the latter carelessly, "except that Jim picked it off the stage."

"And a damned bad job, too," growled he of the beard. "Where's he goin' to fence her up in a corral like this?"

"Bad job, your eye!" answered one who leaned far over to glance at her partially concealed face. "She's a looker, boys . . . she's a regular Cleopatra."

They grouped closely around her.

"Wake her," suggested one, "so's we can size her up."

One who stood closer stirred her rudely with his foot. She sat up, yawning, rubbing her eyes, and smiled up to their faces.

"Turn me into a wall-eyed cayuse," muttered one of them, but the others were silent while their eyes drank.

Montana Pete, with a mop of tawny hair falling low down on his forehead, dropped to a squatting position, the better to look into her eyes.

"Well, baby blue-eyes" — He grinned. — "what d'you think of your new pals?"

"Oh," she cried, with a semblance of pretty confusion, "I . . . I . . . where am I? Oh, I remember."

"Boys," said Montana Pete, rising, "we ain't the kind to have a king, but I'm all for a queen. What?"

"Sure," said the Doctor. "There ain't nothing like the woman's touch to make a home."

They roared with laughter.

"Look out! She's remembering some more, and here comes the waterfall!" called another.

Jerry, in order to get time to plan her campaign, broke into heart-rending sobs.

The bearded man, who rejoiced in the name of Porky Martin, now came forward again. "Lemme take care of her," he said. "I had two mothers, six sisters, an' fourteen sweethearts. I know all about women." He dropped to one knee and put his arm around her. "Take it easy, kid. You're runnin' loose now, an' we'll give you all the rope you want, except enough for hangin' yourself. Look around you, kid, here's enough men to make a jury, and you got a home with every one. Am I right, boys?"

"Let me . . . alone!" wailed Jerry, and she shuddered under the caress.

"Huh?" growled Porky Martin. "She's proud, damn her."

"Give her time, give her time," said the Doctor. "The kid's hurt. She don't savvy yet, boys, that she's in a real democracy where everything's common property."

"No more foolin'," advised Montana Pete. "Jim'll be coming back any time. He'll sure be glad to find us here, I guess not."

"Who's Black Jim?" snarled Porky Martin. "I've stood for enough of his nutty ideas. I say to hell with Black Jim. We've had enough of him!"

"Say that to him," said Montana easily. "I won't hold your hands, Porky. Take it easy, kid" — this to Jerry — "we ain't all swine."

"What d'ya mean?" said Porky in a rising voice.

Jerry trembled, for she knew that, if the men began fighting over her, her fate was sealed.

"You ain't deer, I reckon," said Montana Pete with obvious scorn.

"Let me go!" cried Jerry, not that she hoped for freedom, but because she thought there was some chance of changing the issue. "Let me go! I won't tell about you! I swear I won't!" She extended her hands, one slender and white, and then the other in its ominously stained bandage, first to Porky Martin and then to Pete.

"Look at that," said Pete. "We're a fine gang to stand around makin' life hell for the kid." He dropped to one knee beside her. "We'll give you a square deal, you lay to that, but we can't let you go. There ain't no hope of that, understand."

She shrank against the wall, her sobs coming heavily at intervals.

"What I say is this," orated Porky Martin. "What do you make out of Jim bringin' in two people in one day . . . and one of them a woman?"

40

"Why, you poor fathead," said the Doctor soothingly. "Mac over there was blockin' one of Jim's plays, an', to get him out of the way, Jim took him up here. Anyway, Mac's one of us. What's bitin' you? She was hurt. Besides, maybe Jim wanted that woman's touch around his house."

"Aye," said Porky, "but there's a lot more to be said about that. As far as I go, I'm sick of this feller who stays away from the rest of us . . . never even gets drunk with us . . . and now he gets a woman."

"Look out!" warned a voice. "I think . . ."

Several heads turned to the open door that framed Black Jim. His eyes ran slowly from face to face until they settled on Montgomery. The men stirred uneasily.

"I told you-all to keep these out," he said calmly to Montgomery. By his contemptuous gesture he might have been referring to dogs of the street.

"They said you'd changed your mind," Montgomery explained.

"I ain't ever done that yet," said the bandit. "Hope you've enjoyed yourselves, boys."

"Look here," said Porky Martin, blustering. "What we want to know is about the calico here . . . we . . ."

"I told you about her before," said Black Jim softly, "and you sat around an' hollered an' said she was to stay here. It's too late to get rid of her now. She's seen us all. She could identify every one of us."

"We ain't askin' you to send her off," said Porky, "but as long as she's goin' to stay here, we don't see no nacheral reason why she has to hang around here in

41

one cabin. We're boostin' for a lot of changes of scenery."

"We?" asked Black Jim, and he frowned.

"You heard me before, damn you!" Porky was half crouched with the fighting fury in his face. The rest of the men moved quickly back, leaving an open space between the two. His hand tugged and writhed about the handle of his revolver as though he found difficulty in drawing it, but Black Jim made no movement toward his weapon. His soft, dark eyes dwelt without change on the face of his opponent. Jerry watched, utterly fascinated. She saw Montgomery staring in the background. The rest of the men stood closer to Porky, as if they sympathized with him, and their eyes were fixed with a sort of mute horror on Black Jim. An instinct told her that the moment he made a motion toward his revolver every gun in the room would be out and leveled at him. Yet, when the strange sympathy troubled her throat, it was not for the bandit who faced the roomful of enemies, but for the crouched, tense figure of Porky Martin. His big beard quivered. She saw his jaw stir. A strange, gurgling sound came in his throat, and yet he could not draw his revolver.

"My God," breathed the Doctor.

It was as if some spell broke with his voice. A dozen breaths were audible in quick succession. Porky Martin drew a long pace back and half straightened. His hand left the butt of his revolver, and then both hands moved in slow jerks up toward his head. The gurgling rose louder in his throat. It formed into gasping words.

42

"Jim . . . don't shoot . . . for God's sake!"

The whole of that great body shook. A moment before he had been the most awe-inspiring of them all, and the center of Jerry's fears.

"Hypnotism," she murmured to herself, but she did not believe her own diagnosis.

"Take your hands down, Porky," said Black Jim. "I ain't asked you to put 'em up there."

In spite of this permission, the big man's arms remained as if fixed in air.

"Get out," ordered Black Jim, and gestured toward the door.

Porky started sidewise, edging past Black Jim as if he feared to take his eyes off him. At the door he whirled and bolted suddenly into the dark. The order of the bandit had apparently been directed at Porky alone, but all the rest obeyed, each man moving silently, keeping his face with religious earnestness toward Jim and his hand on his revolver until he came to the door through which each vanished with startling swiftness. They were all gone. Montgomery alone remained. Jim faced him.

"Get out," said the bandit, "an' tell the rest of 'em that there's a deadline drawn at the edge of the trees. They can cross it, when they get tired of livin'."

Jerry made vain motions to him with lips and hands to stay and wondered why she dared not speak out, but his eyes were not for her. Like the rest he moved sidewise, and darted out into the night. Black Jim turned to Jerry, and she set her teeth to make her glance cross his boldly. There was a subtle change in his expression. He jerked a hand toward the door.

"That last man," he said, "did you really want him to stay?"

"Yes," she said faintly, "I'm afraid."

To her astonishment he nodded slowly. "Yes," he said, "they-all ain't much more'n cattle."

With that he disappeared into the next room. He came back at once, bearing a holstered revolver that he dropped beside her carelessly.

"They're a rotten gang, all right," he went on "and that last man . . . why did you want him to stay?"

Under the direct question of his eyes, her own dropped till they fell upon the revolver butt, significantly protruding from the holster.

"You don't need to tell me," he said gently. "I guess you thought you'd be safer with two. But that pale-faced one ain't a man. He's a skunk. I told him to keep 'em out."

She did not answer. Her head remained bowed with wonder. Montgomery had been no protection to her. Even now there were twelve grim men who were twelve dangers to her. Yet, in the presence of this man-queller, she felt unutterably safe. She glanced at her injured hand and smiled at her sense of security. Black Jim retreated. He came back with a great armful of logs.

Hunger and weariness fought like drugs against the stimulus of fear. She found herself drowsing as she stared into the growing blaze of flames. Her ear caught the chink, the rattle, and the hiss of cookery. Then she watched as through a haze the tall figure of Black Jim, swart against the fire. Through her exhaustion, her suffering, and her fear, that shadowy figure became the symbol of the protector.

CHAPTER
SIX

"Greek Meets Greek"

He came before her again, carrying a tin plate mat bore a steaming venison steak flanked with big chunks of bread and a cup of black coffee. She tasted the coffee first, and it cleared her mind, pumped strong blood through her body again. Another woman would have roused to a paralyzing terror, when her faculties returned, but she was used to men and she was not used to the fear of them. After all, what difference was there between this man and those she had known before? She had felt helpless, indeed, when the twelve filled the room. She had seen, and she should never forget a certain flickering light of hunger in their eyes. They were dangerous, but that element of danger she did not see in Black Jim. Some men are dangerous to men alone. Others threaten all nature, born destroyers. She knew that Black Jim was of the first category. Nothing told her except a small inner voice that chanted courage to her heart. Consequently, when the hot coffee gave her strength, she sat erect, propping herself with her sound hand.

"I say!" she called. He started where he sat before his food at the table, lifted his head, and stared at her.

"What about these hobbles, dearie?" she went on. His eyes widened, but he answered nothing. "Cut out the silent treatment, cutie," said Jerry, her courage rising, "and this rope. You've got your stage guarded. There's no fear that I'll jump through the curtain to get to the audience. I can't run away. I'm not very slow, but bullets are a little faster. So drop the hobbles, Alexander. They're way out of date."

He sat with knife poised and ear canted a trifle to one side as if he strained every effort to follow the meaning of her slang. At last he comprehended, nodded, and set her free with a few strokes of a knife.

"It's all right to let you go free," he said, "but you got to remember that this shack may be watched from now on. You could get away any time. I won't stop you. Outside you'll find maybe no bullets, but some of the boys who were in here a while ago. Savvy?"

She understood, but she shrugged the terror away, as she would have shrugged away self-consciousness on the stage.

"All right, Jimmy," she said cheerfully, "I savvy. Lend me a hand, will you?"

She reached up with a smile for him to assist her to her feet. His astonishment at this familiar treatment made his eyes big again, and Jerry laughed.

"It's all right, cutie," she said. "You've got a funny name, but you can't get by as a nightmare as far as I'm concerned. Not without make-up. Can the glassy eye, and give me your hand."

He extended his hand hesitatingly, and she drew herself erect with some difficulty, for she had remained a long time in a cramped position.

"It's all right to feed some Swede farmhand in the corner, Oscar, but not La Belle Geraldine. Nix. It isn't done. There's no red light on that table, is there?"

"Red light?" he repeated.

"Sure. I mean there's no danger sign. Say, dearie, do I have to translate everything I say into Mother Goose rhymes? I mean, may I eat at the table, or do I have to stay on the floor?"

He regarded her a moment with his usual somber concern. Then he turned and carried a stool to the table and brought her food to it.

"This is solid comfort," declared Jerry, as she settled herself at the board, and she attacked the venison with great vigor.

There were certain difficulties, however, against which she had to struggle. Her right hand was useless to manage the knife, but she was able to steady the fork between the third and fourth fingers. With her left hand she tried to cut the meat, but progress in this way was highly unsatisfactory. In the midst of her labors a brawny hand carried away her plate.

She looked up with a laugh and surrendered her knife and fork.

"After all," she said, "you flashed the gun that put my hand to the bad. So it's up to you to do the prompting when I break down."

He raised his eyes a moment to consider this statement, but he failed to find the clue to its meaning, went on silently cutting up the meat, and finally passed it back to her. Dumb-founded by this reticence, Jerry kept a suspicious eye upon him. Among the people with whom she was familiar, silence meant anger, plots, hatred. Evidently he turned the matter over seriously in his mind, for his gaze was fixed far away.

"Lady," he said at last, meeting her inquiry with his dull, unreadable eyes, "was you-all born with that vocabulary, or did you jest find it?"

Jerry rested her chin upon a clenched white fist while she smiled at him. "You're wrong twice, Solomon," she answered. "An angel slipped it to me in a dream."

"A dream like that is some nightmare," nodded Black Jim. "Would you-all mind wakin' up when you talk to me?" He chuckled softly.

"Say, Oscar," said Jerry, "I'd lay a bet that's the first time you've laughed this year."

He was sober at once. "Why?"

"The wrinkles around your eyes ain't worn very deep."

He shrugged his shoulders and confined his attention to his plate for a time, as if the matter no longer interested him, but, when she had half forgotten it, he resumed, breaking into the midst of her chatter: "Speakin' of wrinkles, you don't look more'n a yearling yourse'f. I would ask, how old are you, ma'am?"

The instinct of the eternal feminine made her parry the question for a moment. "I'm old enough," she answered, "but take it from me, I don't have to wear a wig."

"Hmm," he growled, considering this evasive return. "What I want to know is where you-all got to know so much?"

"Know so much?" repeated Jerry. "On the level, Oscar, or speaking with a smile? I mean, do you ask that straight?"

"Straight as I shoot," he said.

She leaned back, curiosity greater than her mirth. "Honest," said La Belle Geraldine, "you've got me beat. You've got me feeling like a toe dancer in the mud. You're the original mystery, all right. To hear people talk of you, you'd think Black Jim put the damn in death. But if I just met you at a dance, I'd think you were so green you didn't know the first violin from the drummer."

"Speakin' in general," replied the bandit carefully, "I get your drift, but even if I begin allowing for the wind . . ."

"Meaning the way I talk, I suppose," broke in Jerry.

"Even allowin' for that," went on Black Jim, "I don't think I could shoot straight enough to ring the bell. You've got me side-stepped."

"Go on," said Jerry, "I'll keep them amused till you bring on the heavy stuff. What do you mean?"

"Well," drawled Black Jim, "you look a heap more like a picture of a lady I once saw in a soap ad than anything else. You're all pink an' white an' soft, with eyes like a two-day calf."

"Go right on, Shakespeare," murmured La Belle Geraldine. "You can't make me mad."

"When I brought you up here," said Black Jim, "I figured that, when you come to, you'd begin yellin' an'

50

hollerin' an' raisin' Cain. I was sort of steelin' myself to it when you opened your eyes a while ago. Lady . . ." — here he leaned across the table earnestly — "I was expectin' a plumb hell of a time." He grinned broadly. "I got it, all right, but not the kind I thought."

"I sure panned you some," nodded Jerry. "I thought . . ." She stopped. To tell Black Jim that she thought she was talking to Frederick Montgomery when she recovered from her faint would be to expose that worthy. Once it were known that he was only a temporary bandit, his days in the valley would be short, indeed. In his pose as a man-killer, an ex-convict, a felon in the shadow of the law, he was as safe as a child in the bosom of his family. Otherwise, a dozen practiced fighters would be hot on his trail. "I was just sore," concluded La Belle Geraldine, "to think I had balled up everything by flashing a small-time act on a big-time stage."

The pun amused her so that she broke into hearty laughter. The sound reacted on both her and the bandit. Although he fell silent again and scarcely spoke for the next hour or more, she thought that she could detect a greater kindliness about his eyes.

He went about cleaning up the tin dishes with singular deftness. When he concluded, he turned abruptly upon her.

"Time to turn in. You sleep there. I bunk in the next room. S'long." He turned at the entrance of the other apartment. "How's your hand?"

"Doing fine," smiled Jerry. "S'long, Jim."

CHAPTER
SEVEN

"Jerry Takes Lessons"

She was still smiling when she slipped down among the blankets. For some time she lay there wondering. By all the laws of Nature she should not have closed an eye for anxiety. She pictured all the dangers of her position, one by one, and then — smiled again. She could not be afraid of this man. The very terror he inspired in others was a warm sense of protection around her. The weary muscles of her body relaxed by slow degrees. The wind hummed like a muted violin through the trees outside. She slept.

When she woke, a fire burned brightly again on the hearth, and the room was filled with the savor of fried bacon and steaming coffee. Black Jim sat at the table, draining his tin cup. Jerry sat up with a yawn.

"Hello, Jim!" she called. "Say, this mountain air is all the dope for hard sleeping, what?"

He lowered the cup and smiled back at her. "I'm glad you-all slept well," he drawled, and rose from the table. "I'm goin' off on a bit of a trip today," he said, "but before I go, I want to tell you . . ."

"My name's Geraldine," she answered, "but most people shorten it up to Jerry."

"Which I'd tell a man jest about hits you off," he answered. "You ain't seen much of the valley. I suppose you'll want to explore around a lot, an' you can go as far as you like, but jest pack that shootin' iron with you by way of a friend. Come here to the door and I'll show you how far you can go."

She followed him obediently and, standing at the entrance to the shack, looked out over the silver-misted valley. Four guardian peaks surrounded a gorge about a mile and a half long and half a mile wide, narrowing toward the farther end where the entrance gap could not have been more than a hundred yards in width. The shack of Black Jim huddled against the precipitous wall of rock at the opposite extremity of the valley and stood upon ground higher than the rest of the floor. Great trees rose on all sides, and what she saw was made out through the spaces between these monsters.

"Where are the others?" she asked.

He waved his hand in a generous circle. "All around. Maybe you could wander about for a month and never find where they stay. But if you meet 'em, they'll be gladder to see you than you'll be to see them."

"If I stay right here," she asked him, "would I be in danger from them?"

"They came last night," he said grimly, "but I got an idea they won't be in no hurry to come again. At the edge of those trees is a deadline. They know if they come beyond that, they're takin' their own chances. If you see 'em come, make your gun talk for you."

He stepped through the door, and she followed him a pace into the open air. The big roan horse, lean of neck and powerful of shoulder, stood near, his bridle reins hanging over his head. Black Jim swung into the saddle.

"Jest hobble this one idea so it don't never get outside your brain," he said. "The men in this valley are only up here because they wanted to get above the law . . . and they are above it. The only law they know, the only law I know, is to play square with each other. Partner, I've busted that law by bringin' you in here. Accordin' to all the rules, there ain't no place for anyone here exceptin' the men that's beyond the law. I dunno what they'll do. Maybe it's war. Maybe it ain't. Rope that idea and stick a brand on it. S'long, Jerry. An' don't get near that gap down to the far end of the valley."

He spurred the roan through the trees and disappeared, leaving Jerry to listen to the rapidly diminishing sound of the horse's hoofs. Then the silence dropped like a cloak about her, save for the light humming of the wind through the upper branches. She went back and buckled the revolver with its holster about her waist. She felt strangely as if that act placed her at once among the ranks of those who — as Black Jim said — were "above the law."

A great impulse to collapse in the middle of the floor and weep rose in her. All that life of gaiety, of action, of many butterfly hopes was lost to her. Years might pass before she could break away from this valley of the damned. Perhaps she might actually grow old here, away from men, away from the lure of the footlights. Hopelessness tightened about her heart, and Jerry began to sing while the tears ran down her face. After all, she was trained to fight against misery, and she fought now until the tears stopped and her voice was sure. The very sound of the song was a cure to all ills.

She set about examining the cabin with the practical mind of anyone who had had to make a home of a dressing room in a theater and who can give a domestic touch even to a compartment in a Pullman. The main room could be made more attractive. When her hand healed, she could cut some young evergreens and place them here and there. That floor could be cleaned. Those clothes, if they had to hang on the wall, might at least be shaken free from dust and covered with sacking. She turned her attention to the adjoining room.

Here was the bunk of Black Jim, covered with a few tumbled blankets. Another pair of lanterns sat in a corner. More clothes lay here and there about the floor. Beyond his room lay the horse shed. She turned back to examine Jim's belongings. What caught her eye was a little pile of books upon a rudely made shelf. She took them down one by one. Here was the explanation of the bandit's mixed English, sometimes almost scholarly and correct, but again full of Western vernacular. It was a cross between the slang of cowboy and mountaineer and the vocabulary of the educated. There were six volumes all told. The first she opened was Scott's RED GAUNTLET which fell open at "Wandering Willie's Tale." Next came a volume of Shakespeare's greatest tragedies — *Othello, Macbeth, King Lear,* and *Hamlet* — then GIL BLAS, a volume of Poe's verse, and another of Byron's, and finally quaint old Malory's

MORTE D'ARTHUR. "Can you beat it?" whispered Jerry to the blank wall. "And me . . . I haven't read a single one of 'em."

How he had got them she could not imagine. Perhaps he had taken them with other loot from a stage. At any rate, they were here, and their presence made her strangely ill at ease. There is a peculiar reverence for books in the minds of the most illiterate. It is a superstition which runs back to the days when the written word had to be copied by hand and a man was esteemed rich if he possessed three or four manuscripts. That legendary reverence grew almost to worship in the early Renaissance, and, when the invention of John Fust finally brought literature within the grasp of the poorest man, the early respect still clung to ink and paper — clings to it today.

Of books Jerry knew little enough and, consequently, had the greater respect. In school she had gone as far as *The Merchant of Venice*, but blank verse was an impassable fence that stood between her and the dramatic action. When she started out on her own gay path through the world, she found small time for reading and less desire. Books were all very well, and the knowledge which might be found in them was doubtless desirable, but for Jerry as unattainable as the shining limousines which purred down Fifth Avenue.

Her first impulse, when she saw this little array of books, was a blind anger whose cause she could scarcely discover. It seemed as if the reading of those books had suddenly placed the bandit as far away from her as he was away from the law. But when the anger died away, a tingling excitement followed. Perhaps through these books she could gain the clue to the inner nature of Black Jim. If these were his only books, he might be molded by the thoughts he found in them. Therefore, through them, she might gain a power over him that, in the end, would avail to bring her safely from the valley. With this purpose before her, Jerry formulated a plan of campaign.

She must in the first place make the bandit like her. When this was done, all things would be possible. But she also knew there was much work before her until this end could be accomplished. His gentleness had not deceived her. It was the velvet touch of the panther's foot with the steel-sharp claws concealed. Those claws would be out and at her throat the moment she attempted an escape, or even a rash movement. In the meantime, she must work carefully, patiently, to win first his respect, and then, perhaps, his affection. It was dangerous to attempt this. Yet it was necessary, and once this was done much might be accomplished. Possibly she could persuade him to attempt flight with her. If so, there was a ghost of a chance he might be able to fight off the rest of the bandits and take her away from the valley.

The eyes of Jerry brightened again with even this faint hope to urge her on. All that day she did what she could, with her one hand, to clean and arrange the rooms. By nightfall she was utterly weary but expectant. The expectancy was vain. Black Jim arrived long after dark, and she heard him moving about in the shed as he put up his roan. It was her signal to commence the cooking of supper. She waited with bated breath for his entrance and his shout of surprise when he saw the changes she had worked in a single day, but, when he did come, it was in silence. He gave no heed either to her or her work.

Jerry fumed in quiet as long as she could, then her plans and resolutions gave way before anger. She dropped a big pan, clatteringly, to the floor. Black Jim, who sat near a lantern at a table reading and calmly waiting for his meal, did not raise his head from his book.

"Say, Lord Algernon," she cried, "wake up and slide your eye over this room! Am I your hired cook, maybe? Am *I* the scrubwoman at eight per?"

He let a vague and unseeing eye rove toward her, and was immediately lost in his book again. She repressed a slight desire to pick up the pan from the floor and hurl it at him.

"All right, dearie," she said, "go on dreaming this is a play, but the *finale* is going to take you off your feet. The silent treatment is OK for some, cutie, but, if you keep it up on me, this show will turn out wilder than a night of UNCLE TOM'S CABIN down in New Orleans."

She resumed her cooking in silence. Black Jim had not favored her with even a glance during this oration. That evening was a symbol of the days to come. He ate in silence, without thanks or regard to her. Apparently, now that her wound was no longer troubling her greatly, his attitude was changed. She felt it was not that he was indifferent. She had simply vanished from his mind. He had cared for her hurt. He had warned her of the dangers she might find in the valley. He had armed her against them. Thereafter, she ceased to occupy his thoughts, for his code was fulfilled.

She fumed and fretted under this treatment at first, but still attempted to follow out her original campaign of winning Black Jim to her side. In all respects she failed miserably. She attempted to read his books. The verse wearied her. The vulgarity of GIL BLAS stopped her in twenty pages. She could not wade through the opening exchange of letters in RED GAUNTLET. Her mind turned back to Montgomery many times during the first ten days, but he never appeared, and then she forgot him.

Black Jim was never at home during the day. He either rode out on the roan or else he went off on foot and returned at night with game, so that they never lacked meat. Cooking, short walks through the trees, endless silences, these things occupied the mind of La Belle Geraldine.

Yet she was not unhappy. She was of the nature that loves extremes, and to her own astonishment, growing every day, she discovered that the hush of the mountains filled her life even more than the clattering gaiety of the stage. Slight, murmuring sounds which would scarcely have reached her ear a month before, now came to her with meaning — the thousand faint stirs that never cease in the forest. Heretofore she had never had a thought which she did not speak. Now she learned the most profound wisdom of all — when the mind speaks to itself and the voice is still.

Whatever of the old restless activity remained in her found a vent in the ceaseless study of the bandit. She picked up a thousand clues, little by little, but they all led in different directions. At the end of a month she felt she was further away from the truth than she had been at the first. All that she really knew was what he had told her. He lived above the law. She knew him well enough to see he was not a criminal because of hate for other men, or even because he loved the thrill of his night riding. He simply avoided that other world of men because it was a world where life was constrained by a thousand rules.

To her mind, he was like a powerful and sinisterly beautiful beast of prey that hunts where it will through the forest and, when it is pressed in its haunts by man, turns and strikes him down. She carried the animal metaphor still further. She saw it in his singular silence, which was not reticence, but the speechlessness of a man to whom words are of no use. She saw it most of all in the singularly fathomless eyes. They never mocked her. They were simply veils through which she could not look.

The face changes expression only because man lives among fellows whom he wishes to read his emotions, his anger, his pleasure, his contempt. Therefore, his features grow mobile. Black Jim lived alone. When he was with men and wished to express an emotion, he did not pause to express his will in anything save action. At first, when the endless chatter of La Belle Geraldine disturbed him of an evening, he simply rose and left the cabin to walk through the woods. It was not long before she understood why.

The clock which ticks out our lives in the cities of men had no place in his house. He rose in the morning early because, like an animal again, he could not sleep after the light came. He felt no measuring of time by which to check and control his actions. He ate at any hour, now and then, once a day, often four times. Jerry fell into his habits through the strong force of a near example. The ticking of the clock no longer entered her consciousness and, in its place, flowed the broad and tideless river of life.

CHAPTER
EIGHT

"The Sign Of The Beast"

The deadline that Black Jim said he had drawn around his cabin certainly had its effect, for never after the first day did she see one of the bandits. Now and again she caught the sound of distant firing when they practiced with their guns. Three or four times she heard drunken singing through the night as they held high festival. Otherwise, she knew naught of them or their actions, although her mind retained the grim gallery of their portraits. The day would surely be when Black Jim should fail to return from one of his expeditions, and then . . . ?

That day came. She waited till late at night, but he did not appear. She could scarcely sleep, and, when the morning came, she sat in the cabin, guessing at a thousand horrors. A voice took up a song in the distance, and then came closer and closer. Jerry stood up and felt for her revolver with a nervous hand. The voice rose clearer and clearer. She could make out the words:

Julia, you are peculiar;
Julia, you are queer.

Jerry dropped her hands on her hips and drew a long breath, partly of vexation and partly of relief.

"It's Freddie," she muttered.

> Truly, you are unruly,
> As a wild Western steer.
> Some day, when we marry,
> Dear one, you and I;
> Julia, you little mule, you,
> I'm going to rule you,
> Or die.

The song ended as the singer approached the edge of the open space before Black Jim's cabin. Jerry stepped through the door to see Montgomery standing in the shadow of the trees.

"Yea, Jerry!" he yelled. "Is the gunman around?"

"He's not here," she answered. "You don't have to be afraid of anything, Freddie."

"Oh, don't I?" came the reply. "Didn't he make this a deadline, La Belle Geraldine? Suppose he should come back and find me on the other side of it? Not me, Jerry. I like life too well!"

"Where've you been?" said Jerry, approaching him, "and what in the *world* have you been doing, Freddie?"

For as she drew closer she found herself looking upon a Frederick Montgomery who, voice alone, remained the man she had known. A vast stubble of black beard and whiskers, unshaven for full two weeks or more, obscured the fine outline of his features. His broad hat, pushed back from his forehead, allowed a mop of tangled hair to fall down almost to his eyes. Overalls, soiled and marred with wrinkles, a shirt torn savagely across the side, muddy boots, and the heavy revolver completed his equipment. Jerry was aghast.

"What's the matter?" asked Montgomery. "Some hit, this costume, eh? It isn't make-up, kid. It's the real thing."

"And I suppose you're the real thing under it?" said Jerry in deep disgust.

"Sure," he said easily. "Stack all your chips and put 'em on me, kid. I'm the real stuff."

"Why haven't you been around?" asked Jerry sharply, and bitter anger took her breath. "You knew I was left here at the mercy of Black Jim. You haven't done a thing to help me! Why?"

"Why?" repeated the other, but not peculiarly embarrassed. "There's a reason, kid. I've been too busy living."

"Too busy getting dirty, you mean," snorted La Belle Geraldine. "Go make yourself decent and then come back, if you want to talk with me. But if you've got dirt in your mind, Freddie, water won't help you."

He growled deep in his throat, and she stepped back a pace. She had never heard such an ominous sound from him before; now she scanned him more closely. It seemed to her that his eyes were sunken and shadowed significantly.

"Don't try that line on me any more, Jerry," he answered. "You could get by in the old days, but it won't do up here."

"Won't it, dearie?" asked Jerry with a rather dangerous sweetness.

"Not a hope, kid," he answered. "I'm through with all that stuff. Down in the States a jane could pull that line now and then and get by with it, but up here it's a man's country, and it's up to you to side-step when anything in pants comes along."

"As a man," returned Jerry — yet for some reason she did not feel as brave as her words — "as a man, cutie, you come about as close to the real article as make-up will let you. But I'm behind the scenes, and it won't quite do, Mister Montgomery, it won't quite do."

He scowled, but he softened his tone as he answered. "Look here, Jerry," he said, "I didn't come here looking for a fight. Am I your friend or am I not?"

"Do you remember how you backed out of the room when Black Jim simply looked at you, Freddie?" she asked gently.

"Sure I do," he growled, "but you can't hold that against me, Jerry. There isn't a man of the bunch who would take a chance face to face with Black Jim. He ain't human, you ought to know that. The only difference between him and a tiger is that he uses a gun. He's just . . ."

"Cut it out, Freddie," she broke in. "I'm tired of you already. Ring off. Hang up. You're on the wrong wire."

"Say, kid," he said with gravity, "do I gather that you stand for that man-eater?"

"Take it any way you like," she said coldly.

He laughed. "Of course, you don't," he went on disagreeably. "You're simply kidding me along. What if

I could show you the way out of the valley tonight, Jerry?"

She caught her breath. "The way out? Freddie! Are you playing me straight?"

"I don't know," he said with a trace of sullenness, "but this is my night on duty at the gap."

"Then I'm free!" she cried. "I'll start as soon as it's pitch dark and . . ."

"Wait a minute," he interrupted, "don't run away with yourself. If you disappeared, Black Jim would know I let you pass, and, when he found out that his . . ."

"Stop there," she said. "Freddie, what do you mean . . . do you think . . . ?"

"Lay off on that, Jerry," returned Montgomery. "You're a swell dancer, but you can't get away with heavy stuff like this. You've been all alone with him here, haven't you?"

She touched her hand to her forehead and wondered at its coldness in a vague way. "Why should I care?" she murmured. "Let him think what he will."

"But I'm still strong for you," Montgomery was saying. "Don't get white and scared, kid. I don't hold it against you much. What I say is . . . why not get rid of Black Jim? You can take him off his guard. Say the word, and I'll hang around at night, and you can signal me when he's asleep. Then I'll come and do the work. It'd be a risky job, but for your sake, kid, I'd . . ."

"You've said enough," she answered, summoning her courage and fighting back her disgust, for here was her one chance to gain freedom. "If you're afraid of him, why not go with me? What's your idea? Do you really intend to stay here? Freddie, you haven't become one of those swine!"

He laughed heavily. "Swine?" he repeated. "Say, kid, did you ever see swine with this stuff hanging around in their hides?" He slid a hand into his hip pocket and brought it out again full of gold pieces of three denominations. He poured it deftly back and forth. "Take a slant at it, Jerry. Listen to 'em click. One little job I pulled last week brought me this and about twice as much more. Easy? Say, it's a shame to take the coin. It's like robbing the cradle. Do you think I'd leave this game even to go off with you, Jerry? Not till I'm blind, kid. Get wise! Say the word, and we can pull a stunt on Black Jim that'll give us the cabin and all the loot stacked up in it." His eyes glittered. "How much *has* he got stowed away in there, kid?"

She retreated another pace. He was half a dozen yards away now.

"I don't know," she murmured. Fear was growing in her, and horror with it. In sudden desperation she held out her hand to him and cried: "Freddie, what is it? You were pretty clean when you first came up here. What has changed you? What's happened?"

"What's happened?" he asked dully, as if he could not follow her meaning.

"Yes, yes! Open your lungs . . . taste this air. Isn't that enough in itself to make a man of you? And the scent of the evergreen, Freddie . . . and the nearness of the sky . . . and the whiteness of the stars . . ."

"And the absence of the law, kid," he broke in. "Don't forget that. A man makes his own law up here, which means no law at all. We're above it, that's what we are. Stay here a little longer, and you'll get it, too."

She stared at him with great eyes, while her mind moved quickly. She was beginning to understand, not the gross-minded brute that Frederick Montgomery had become, but the singular influence of the wild free life. Of those other twelve and of Montgomery, the open license made animals. There *was* a difference between them and Black Jim. She had felt the touch of the animal in him, too, but in another manner. The others were like feeders on carrion. He was truly a great and fearless beast of prey. The solemn silences of the mountains imparted to him some of their own dignity. The mystery and the terror of the wilderness were his.

"Above the law?" she said. "No, you're beneath it. I wish . . . I wish I were a man for half a minute . . . to rid the world of you all!" She turned and fled back to the cabin.

"Jerry! Oh, Jerry!" he shouted from the edge of the clearing where the deadline of Black Jim still held him.

She turned at the door.

"Have you made up your mind about it finally?" he asked.

She shuddered so, she could not answer.

"Then, by God, I'll have you, if I have to get Black Jim first, and I'll get his other loot when I get you!"

He disappeared among the trees, and she went back into the cabin, weak at heart and filled now with a strange yearning for the return of Black Jim. The

68

vultures, she felt, circled above the valley, waiting for her. He was the strong eagle that would put them to flight.

Evening drew on. He did not come. Night settled black over the valley, and the white stars brushed the great trees that fringed the cliffs. Still he did not come. The hearth fire remained unlighted. The damp cold of darkness numbed her hands and her heart. She waited, bowed and miserable. He was delayed, but delay to Black Jim could mean only death. No other force could take all this time for his return. This grew more certain as the hours passed. In that gloom every minute meant more than whole hours during the day.

At last she made up her mind. Montgomery — not the light-hearted man she had known, but a hot-eyed beast — threatened her. Not he alone, but perhaps all of the other twelve were so many dangers. Now that Black Jim was gone, she was helpless in their hands. By the next day they would know of his long absence and come for her — for her and for the rest of the loot, as Montgomery had said. She must get away from the valley that night.

The sentinel was there, to be sure, but that sentinel was Montgomery, and she felt there was a fighting chance she could pass him safely in the gap. If necessary, she could fight, and perhaps she could handle a revolver as well as he. Perhaps she could surprise him. He would not be expecting it, and, if she could get him under the aim of her revolver, she knew he would not play the role of hero. Once out of the gap there was an even chance for life. She might wander through the mountains until she starved to death. On the other hand she might find a road and follow it to town. She weighed the chances in her own practical way, rose from the stool, saw that her cartridge belt was well filled, strapped a canvas bag full of food on the other hip, and left the cabin.

She kept as closely as possible to the center of the valley, for she felt that the habitations of the gang must lie close to the wall, on which side she could not know. As she approached the gap, she went more and more slowly, for here the valley began to narrow rapidly, and the chance she might encounter one of the twelve grew greater. At every step she feared a discovery, for it was impossible to guess what lay immediately before her. The valley floor was not only thick with great trees, but mighty boulders. They had evidently been split by erosion from the cliffs around and lay here and there, a perfect hiding place for a veritable army. The keen scent of woodsmoke reached her nostrils. She paused a moment, uncertain from which direction it came, for the air was still. Then she turned to the right and stole on with careful steps. Each crackling of a twig beneath her feet made her heart thunder.

CHAPTER
NINE

"Jerry Decides"

The scent of smoke grew fainter, ceased, and came again. A murmur like the sound of a voice brought her to a dead halt to listen. She heard nothing further for a moment, and went on again until a great rock, full forty feet in height, blocked her progress, and she began to circle it. As she turned a corner of the great rock, she stopped short, and dropped to the ground. The big rock and several smaller ones close to it lay in a rough circle, and in the center of the space smoked a pile of wood that would soon break into flames. Already little crimson tongues licked along the edges, quivered, and went out, to be replaced by others. By the dim light of this rising fire, she made out shadowy figures one after another — nine in all — and could not see all of the circle.

"Start it yourself, Porky," said a voice.

A snatch of flame jerked up the side of the pile of wood and flickered a moment like a detached thing at the top. By that light she saw the big, bearded fellow leaning against a rock just opposite her.

"Not me," he answered. "Mac will be back, maybe. If he don't come, I'll start the ball rollin'. Gimme time."

The fear which made her drop to the ground still paralyzed Jerry, so that she heard these things as from a great distance. With all her heart she wished for the strength to creep back from the rock, but for the moment she was incapable of movement. The clatter of a galloping horse drew up to the rocks and stopped. Montgomery entered the circle and threw himself down beside Porky. A general silence held the group. The fire flamed up and showed clearly the round of somber faces as they turned to Montgomery.

New heart came to Jerry, for Montgomery had evidently abandoned his place in the gap, and now the way of her flight lay clear. She rose cautiously from her prone position to her hands and knees and began to draw softly back.

"Did he come through?" asked a voice.

"Just passed me," answered Montgomery, "and he was riding hard. The roan looked as if he'd covered a hundred miles today."

Jerry paused, all ears, and her heart leaped. They must mean that Black Jim had ridden through the pass. The shadow of the rock concealed her perfectly, and unless someone actually walked upon her, through the aperture between the two big boulders, there was practically no chance they could discover her presence. Black Jim had returned, and now she connected his return to the valley, for some unknown reason, with this assemblage in the night. She could not forget the threat that Montgomery had made earlier in the day.

"Put it to them straight, Mac," said Porky to Montgomery. "Give 'em the whole idea, just the way you talked it over with me. They're set to listen. I sort of prepared the way."

"All right," agreed Montgomery. "I'll tell you where I stand. I'm tired as hell of having Black Jim walk all over us. I say, if we're men, we've got to put an end to it, savvy?"

Another of those little ominous silences fell on the circle.

"It appears to me, partner," drawled Montana, "that you're talkin' a powerful lot, when a man might say you're only jest landed among us."

"He ain't askin' you to come in on the plan," broke in Porky aggressively. "Neither am I. Jest listen, an', if you don't like the idea a mighty sight, nobody's goin' to hurt you for staying out."

"Nacherally," agreed the Doctor, "but kick out with your hunch, Mac."

Jerry went cold, yet she edged a little closer for fear that a single, low-pitched word might escape her.

"I haven't been here long," said Montgomery, "but, while I've been here, I've learned enough about Black Jim for him to make me sick."

"He generally makes folks feel that way," said a voice, and a chuckle followed that broke off short, for Porky was glowering from face to face.

"You remember what he did the day after he brought the girl into the valley?"

"I reckon he brought you-all in about the same time," said the man of the pale face and yellow teeth, grinning.

Montgomery frowned back. "He took me from behind," he said savagely. "I didn't have no chance to get at my gun, or maybe the story wouldn't be the same."

"Go on, Silent," encouraged Porky. "Don't let 'em throw you off the trail."

"All right. You remember he came down here and told us all he had a deadline drawn around his cabin at the edge of the trees, and, if any of us crossed it, he was no better than dead meat?"

A general growl rose, for the memory angered them to their hearts.

"We all were pretty still when he spoke," said Montgomery, "and my way of looking at it, we acted like a bunch of whipped dogs."

"Kind of smile when you say that, partner," said the pale-faced man, "or pretty soon, maybe, you'll be riding your idea to death."

"I'm telling you what it seemed to me," said Montgomery. "I say, what right has Black Jim got to make rules up here? This valley is above the law, isn't it?"

"It ain't the first thing he done," said Porky. "He's been makin' laws of his own all the time, an', by God, I ain't the man to stand for it no longer, which I say, Black Jim is always a-bluffin' from a four-flush."

"Me, speakin' personal," added the Doctor, "I got no use for a man that won't liquor up with the boys now an' then. It shows he ain't got any nacheral trust for his pals."

74

"I say it's come to a showdown," said Montgomery. "Either we've got to move out and leave the valley to Black Jim, or he's got to move out and leave it to us. Am I right?"

"All savin' one little thing," drawled a voice. "You-all seem to be forgettin' that Black Jim ain't partic'lar willin' to move for anybody. Ef it comes to movin' him, he'll have to be carried out feet first, in a way of speakin'."

"And why not move him that way?" asked Montgomery.

Once more the breathless silence fell. Jerry could see each man flash a questioning glance at his neighbor, and then each pair of eyes fell, glowering upon the fire. A little, gritting sound caught her, and she found she was grinding her teeth savagely. All her wild, loyal nature revolted against this cool and secret plotting.

"Because it ain't no way possible," said the Doctor, "to ride Black Jim without buckin' straps an' a Spanish bit."

"Maybe not for one man," said Montgomery softly, "but here's twelve that can all shoot straight and every one knows his gun. Can Black Jim stand up against us all at one time?"

"Maybe not," said the Doctor, "but he ain't no gun-shy paint pony, an', before we're through flashin' guns, some of us are goin' to start out on the long trail for the happy huntin' grounds. You can stack your chips on that, partner I"

"Then, by God!" cried Porky, starting to his feet with such suddenness that the others shrank a little. "If you're goin' to quit cold, me an' Silent Mac'll take on the game by ourselves, and we split the loot between us. There'll be a lot of it. He don't never spend it any ways I can see . . . no liquor, no gambling', no nothin'. Boys, the stuff must be piled up to the roof!"

Without hardly knowing what she did, Jerry drew the revolver from her holster and aimed a deadly bead on Porky's breast. She checked herself with horror at the thought that a single pressure of her finger would bring a man to his death. Three or four others rose around the circle.

"If it comes to a showdown, Porky," said one of them, "we'll stack our chips with yours. I'm ag'in' Black Jim, an' I'd jest as soon tell him so from the talkin' end of a gun."

"Me, too," said another, and a clamor of voices rose in affirmation.

Jerry began to draw back, head whirling.

"Then there's no time like tonight," called Montgomery, "and I tell you how we can work best."

He lowered his tone as he spoke, and, as Jerry drew back behind the jutting angle of the rock, she heard only a confused murmur. There she crouched a long moment, thinking as she had never thought before. The way out of the valley lay clear before her. If she rose and walked on, she would be free within ten minutes, and in fifteen escape beyond the reach of pursuit. The other alternative was to turn back to the cabin of Black Jim and warn him of the danger which threatened. If she did this, it meant she would be involved in the same fate that was soon to envelope the solitary bandit.

Thirteen men that night would attack him. When he fell, she would be the prize of the victors. Jerry moaned aloud. Then she rose, still crouching, and hurried off among the trees toward the gap of the valley. Terror drove her faster and faster. When she reached the last rise of ground, she broke into a stumbling run. In another moment she stood at the farther end of a narrow pass, and paused an instant to catch her breath. Before her the ground pitched steeply down, down to freedom. On that outward trail she would be headed again for happiness, for the applause of the gay hundreds, for the shimmer of footlights, that had been to her like signal fires which led finally to fame. She looked back to the valley. It was black as death. She looked up, and there were the cold, white stars, very near. One of them seemed to burn in the top of a tall pine, a lordly tree.

A great weakness mastered Jerry, and she dropped to her knees, her shoulder pressing against the cliff that fenced the gap. Perhaps the thirteen were even then prowling toward the cabin of Black Jim. Perhaps Jim was stooped over the hearth, kindling the fire. Perhaps he even thought of her, at least to wonder carelessly where she had gone. Big tears formed in her eyes and ran hotly down her cheeks. She threw her arms up toward the pallid stars, and her hands were fiercely clenched.

"Oh, God," she said, whispering the words, "tell me what's the big-time thing to do. How'm I going to put over this act right? I've been on the small time so long I don't know what to do. I don't know what to do."

Surely there was an answer to that prayer, for her tears ceased at once. She rose and looked once more longingly down the slope that led to liberty. Then she turned and went back into the double night of the valley. She went on at a swinging step, and hope came to her as she walked. Surely the crew of Porky and Montgomery would deliberate some time longer, laying their plans for the attack. She had heard enough to know they feared Black Jim worse than death, and they would not be the men to take greater chances than necessary. She might reach the cabin before them. Once or twice she started to run, but she stopped and swung into a walk again for she must not exhaust her strength. There might be need for it all, before the night was done.

CHAPTER
TEN

"A Straight Game With A Fixed Deck"

She grew more and more cautious as she approached the farther end of the valley and, for a time, hesitated at the edge of the circle of trees around the cabin, watching and listening. She found nothing suspicious. When she moved a little to one side, she saw a shaft of light fall from a window of the house. It was a golden promise to Jerry, and her heart beat strongly again with hope. Once with Black Jim she felt, at that moment, as if they could fight off the whole world between them.

She went tiptoeing across the open space like a child stealing up to catch a playmate by surprise. At the open door she stood a moment, peeking around the corner and into the interior. The shock of discovery unnerved her even more than the plot she had overheard, scarcely an hour before. By the lantern light she saw Black Jim standing with folded arms beside her bunk. He stared down at an array of woman's clothes that was spread out on the blankets. She saw a long, rose-colored scarf, a dress of blue silk that shimmered faintly in the dim light, light shoes on the floor, a small round hat, and there were other articles at which she could only guess, for they were not all exposed.

"Jim!" she called softly, and then stepped into the doorway.

He whirled with a clutching hand on the butt of his revolver. He was pale, but a deep color poured into his face, and his eyes wavered to the floor under her shining glance. "I thought you were gone," he said. "I thought . . ." He raised his head and went to her with outstretched hand. "Jerry," he said, as she met his grasp, "I was thinkin' a while ago that I didn't care for anything livin' except the roan. But I reckon I'd have missed you."

The confession came forth stammeringly. Jerry pressed his hand in both of hers. "You're just . . . you're just a dear," she said, and in a moment she was on her knees, turning over the finery, article by article. Tears brimmed her eyes again. "I thought you never noticed me," she said, turning to him. "I thought I was no more than the blank wall to you, Jim."

"A man would be blind that didn't see your clothes was getting some worn, Jerry," he said, and she saw that his eyes were traveling slowly over her from head to foot, as if to make sure she had really come back to him. It thrilled her with a happiness different from any ever known in her life. She forgot the danger of the thirteen gangsters and the warning that she had come back to give Black Jim at such a peril to herself. She leaned over the clothes to conceal the hot color in her face and to fight against a sudden sense of self-consciousness. It was more like stage fright than

80

anything else, yet it was different. It was not the fear of many critical eyes. It was an awful knowledge that her own searching vision was turned back upon her soul and every corner of her heart lay exposed. And still that quivering, foolish, childish happiness sang in her like the murmur of a harp string.

She felt a slight touch at her side. Black Jim had opened the canvas bag and glanced at the contents. He stepped back, a frown and a smile fighting on his face.

"You did start on the out trail, Jerry?" he asked.

She remembered now with horrible suddenness all she had come back to tell him. It brought her slowly to her feet, white, tense.

"I *did* start," she answered. "You were gone so long. I thought you were hurt . . . killed . . . and that I was left here at the mercy of . . ." She stopped and then hurried on. "I started to go down the valley, and on the way I came to the same crowd of men who were in this room the night you brought me here. They were around a fire. I hid beside a rock and listened to their talk. They were threatening you, Jim. They plan to come up here tonight and attack you . . . because of the gold you have . . . and me. They were all there. They hadn't even left a man to guard the gap."

"Which left you plumb free to go on out of the valley," said Jim, half to himself, and entirely disregarding the rest of her speech.

"We must leave at once!" she cried. "We must try to sneak off down the valley before they arrive to make their attack . . ."

"But you came back here to tell me," he went on, musing, "when you might have got away."

She caught him by the arm and shook it savagely. "Wake up!" she called. "Listen to me! Don't you understand what's going to happen?"

"I didn't think there was no man would do that," he said, "leastwise, not up here. But now a woman has done it . . . for me." For the wonder of it, he shook his head slowly. "Jerry, I've been considerable of a fool."

"Yea, Jim!" called a voice from the night.

"Git down," whispered Black Jim, and dragged her to the floor. "Keep low when the bullets start comin', an' stay down. Hell is just startin' around here."

"Don't go," she pleaded, clutching him. "They want you to go out, and then they'll shoot at you from the shelter of the trees."

His faint chuckle answered her. "After all, Jerry, I'm not a *plumb* fool!"

He ran softly to the door and swung it open. "Who's there?" he called. Then he whispered to Jerry: "I can see four of them among the trees, an' Montgomery an' Porky are standin' by the deadline, waiting for me to come out. Watch them from the other side of the cabin. They might try to rush from that side."

"Come out!" answered the voice of Montgomery. "We got to see you, Jim, or let us come across your deadline."

Jerry ran to the narrow window on the farther side of the room and peered out cautiously. The new, risen moon shed so faint a light she could see nothing at first.

"What d'you want with me?" she heard Black Jim say.

Now, as she strained her eyes, she made out one, two, three dim figures moving behind the trees. The cabin was surrounded on all sides.

"We need you, Jim," answered Porky's voice. "They's a passel of men camped in the gap. When day comes, they'll start cleanin' out our valley."

Black Jim chuckled. "Jest a minute, boys," he called. "Wait there, an' I'll be with you." He crossed hurriedly to Jerry.

"They're on this side, too, Jim," she breathed. "They have us surrounded. It's death to us both, Jim. There's no escape."

"Remember this," he whispered. His hand closed on her shoulder. "Whatever happens, keep close to the floor. They got us trapped. Maybe there ain't any hope. Anyway, it'll be a fight they'll remember . . ."

"I will. I will," she answered, and her voice trembled, for he seemed to have caught at her whole soul with his hand, "but before it begins . . . I've got to say . . . I've got to tell you . . ." She stopped, then went on with a great effort. "Jim, before we die . . ."

"Hush," he said. "There ain't goin' to be no death for you."

"Before we die," she pressed on, "remember that I love you with all my heart and soul, Jim."

"Jerry, you're talkin' loco."

"It isn't much to be loved by a small-time actress, and I've never once been behind the lights on the real big time. But, oh, Jim, I wish I was keen in the bean like Cissy Loftus, because then . . ."

Slowly, fumblingly, his arms went around her and tightened. "Jerry," he whispered.

"Yes?" she answered in the same tone.

"It seems to me . . ."

"Dear Jim."

"It won't be so partic'lar hard . . ."

"Dear . . . dear old Jim."

"To pass out now. But it's too late to ask for a new deal. This deck's already shuffled and stacked. Jerry, we'll play a straight game, even with a fixed deck. An' . . . an' I love you, honey, more'n the roan an' my six-gun put together." He gathered her close with powerful arms, but the kiss that touched her eyes and then her lips was gentle and reverent.

"Are you sleepin', Jim?" called a voice.

He turned and went with drawn revolver to the door, still ajar. From behind him, Jerry could see Montgomery and Porky standing in the moonlight.

"I ain't sleepin'," replied Black Jim, "but I'm figurin' why I ain't shot such hounds as you two, without warnin'."

As if he had pressed a spring that set automata in motion, they whirled and leaped behind trees.

"Take warning!" called Black Jim. "I could have bagged you both with my eyes shut, an' the next man of you that I see I'll let him have it!"

For reply a revolver barked, and a bullet thudded into the heavy door. Black Jim slammed it and dropped the latch. A series of wild yells sounded from the trees on all sides, and a dozen shots rang in quick succession. After this first venting of their disappointed spleen, the bandits were silent again. Jerry poised her revolver and searched the trees carefully. A hand dropped on her arm, and another hand took away the revolver.

"If there's shootin' to be done," said Black Jim, "I'll do it. The blood of a man don't wash off so easy, even from soft white hands like yours, Jerry."

"Then when you shoot, shoot to kill!" she said fiercely. "They are trying for your life like bloodhounds, Jim."

"Kill?" he repeated, taking up his place at the small window with his revolver raised. "Jerry, I've never killed a man yet, no matter what people say, an' I'm not goin' to begin now. Why, a bullet in the leg or the shoulder puts a man out of the way jest as well as if it went through the heart. Git down closer to the floor."

His gun exploded. A yell from the edge of the trees answered him, and then a chorus of shouts and a score of bullets in swift succession smashed against the logs. Through the silence that followed they heard a distant, faint moaning.

Black Jim, running with his body bent close to the floor, crossed the room to the window on the other side. Almost instantly his gun spoke again, and a man screamed in the night among the trees.

"Too high," she heard Jim saying. "I meant it lower."

"They're beaten, Jim," she called softly. "They don't dare try to rush the cabin. They're beaten."

"Not yet," he answered. "Unless they're plumb crazy, they'll tackle us from the blind side. There ain't any window in the shed, Jerry."

CHAPTER
ELEVEN

"Back To The Law"

From three sides of the house he could command the approaches through the door and the two slits in the wall which answered in place of windows. On the side of the shed, where the roan was stabled, there was not the smallest chink through which he could fire. Jerry sat twisting her hands in despair.

"Take the axe, Jim," she said at last, "and chop away a hole in the logs. They're all light and thin. You could make a place to shoot from in a minute."

He started to fumble about in the dark for the axe. But the weak side of the cabin was too apparent to be overlooked by the besiegers. Before the axe was found, a great crackling of fire commenced outside the shed and a cry of triumph rose from the men without. The sound of the fire rose; the roan whinnied with terror. Black Jim slipped his revolver back into his holster, and turned with folded arms to Jerry.

"So this is *the finale*," she said with white lips. "Where's our soft music and the curtain, Jim?"

"Let the girl out!" shouted the voice of Montgomery. "We won't hurt her! Come out, Jerry!"

"Go on out, honey," said Black Jim.

She went to him and drew his arm about her. "Do you think I'd go out to them, Jim?"

"I don't think," he said. "I know. There's nothin' but death in here."

A gust of wind puffed the flames to a roar up the side of the shed outside, and they heard the stamping of the roan in an agony of panic.

"There's only two ways left to me," she said, "and dying with you is a lot the easiest, Jim. Give back my gun."

"Honey," he said, and she wondered at the gentleness of his voice, "you're jest a girl . . . a bit of a slip of a girl . . . an' I can't noways let you stay in here. Go out the door. They won't shoot."

"Give back my gun," she repeated.

She felt the arm about her tremble, and then the butt of a revolver was placed in her hand. The fire hissed and muttered now on the roof of the cabin. Red glimmers of light showed and filled the interior with a grim dance of shadows.

"I never knew it could be this way, Jerry," he said.

"Nor I, either," she answered, "and the day I make my final exit is the day I really began to live. Jim, it's worth it."

Through another pause they listened to the fire. Outside, Montgomery was imploring the girl to leave the house, and, as the fire mounted, an occasional yell from the crowd applauded its progress.

"Seein' we're goin' out on the long trail together," said Black Jim, "ain't there some way we can hitch up, so's we can be together on the other side of the river?"

She did not understand.

"I mean, supposin' we were married . . ."

She pressed her face against his body to keep back a sob.

"Seems to me," he went on, "that I can remember some of a marriage I once read. Do you suppose, Jerry, that if me an' you said it over now, bein' about to die, that it would mean anything?"

"Yes, yes!" she cried eagerly. "We're above the law, Jim, and what we do is either sacred or damned."

"The part I remember," he said calmly, although the room was hot now with the rising fire, "begins something like this, an' it ain't very long. Is Jerry your real name, honey?"

"My real name is Annie Kerrigan. And yours, Jim?"

"I was never called nothin' but Black Jim. Shall I begin?"

"Yes."

"I, Black Jim, take thee, Annie . . ."

"I, Annie, take thee, Black Jim," she repeated.

"To have and to hold . . ."

"To have and to hold."

"For better or worse . . ."

"For better or worse."

"Till death do us part . . ."

"Jim, dear Jim, can *that* part us?"

"Nothin' between heaven an' hell can, honey. Annie, there was the ring, too, but I ain't got a ring."

The room was bright with the firelight now. She raised her left hand and kissed the third finger. "Jim, dear, this is a new kind of marriage. We don't really need a ring, do we?"

"We'll jest suppose that part."

The roan made the whole cabin tremble with his frantic efforts to break from his halter.

"An' old Roan Bill goes with us," said Black Jim. "Everything I wanted comes with me in the end of things, honey. But he ought to die easier than by fire."

He drew his revolver again and stepped through the doorway into the shed. Jerry followed him and saw Roan Bill standing crouched and shuddering against the wall, his eyes green with fear. Black Jim stepped to him and stroked the broad forehead. For a moment Roan Bill kept his terrified eyes askance upon the burning wall of the shed. Then he turned his head and pressed against Jim, as if to shut out the sight. With his left hand stroking the horse gently along the neck, Jim raised his revolver and touched it to the temple of Roan Bill. Another cry broke from the crowd without, as if they could look through the burning walls and witness the coming tragedy and glory in it.

"Old pal," said Black Jim, "we've seen a mighty pile of things together, an', if hosses get on the other side of the river, I got an idea I'll find you there. So long."

"Wait!" called Jerry. "Don't shoot, Jim."

He turned toward her with a frown as she ran to him.

"The wall, Jim! Look at the wall of the shed!"

The thin wall had burned through in many places, and the wood was charred deeply. In several parts the

90

burning logs had fallen away, leaving an aperture edged with flames.

"I see it," said Black Jim. "It's about to fall. Get back in the cabin."

"Yes," she answered, fairly trembling with excitement, "even a strong puff of wind would blow it in. Listen! I see the ghost of a chance for us. Blindfold Roan Bill so that the fire won't make him mad. We'll both get in the saddle. Then you can beat half of that wall down at a single blow. We'll ride for the woods. They won't be watching very closely from this side. We may . . . we may . . . there's one chance in a thousand."

He stared at her a single instant. Then by way of answer jerked the saddle from a peg on the wall of the cabin and threw it on the roan's back. Jerry darted into the cabin and came out with a long scarf that she tied firmly around the horse's eyes. In two minutes their entire preparations were completed, and a money belt dropped into a saddlebag. Jerry was in the saddle with the roan trembling beneath her, and the reins were clutched tightly in one hand, a revolver in the other. Black Jim caught up a loose log end, fallen from the wall.

"There . . . in the center!" she called. "It's thinnest there!"

"The minute it falls, start the roan," he said. "I'll swing on behind as you pass."

With that he swung the log end around his head and drove it against the wall. A great section fell. He struck again. A yell came from without as another width crushed down, and Jerry loosened the reins. At the very moment that Black Jim caught the back of the saddle, the roan stepped on a red-hot coal and reared away, but Jim kept his hold and was safe behind the saddle as the horse made his first leap beyond the burning timbers.

"They're out! This way!" shouted a voice from the trees, and two shots in quick succession hummed close to them.

Fifty yards away lay the trees and safety. The roan lengthened into a racing stride. A chorus of yells broke out around the house, and Jerry saw a man jump from behind a tree, the flash of a revolver in his hand. The long arm of Black Jim darted out, and his gun spoke once, and again. The man tossed up his arms and pitched forward to the ground. Still another revolver barked directly before them, and she saw, by the light of the flaming house, the great figure of Porky Martin, half hidden by a tree trunk. A bullet tore through the horn of the saddle.

The woods were only a fraction of a second away from them. Martin stood in their path. Once more the revolver of Black Jim belched, and, as they plunged into the saving shadow of the trees, she saw the outlaw stagger and clutch at his throat with both hands.

"To the left . . . to the left," said Black Jim, "and straight down the valley for the gap!"

A week later a golden-haired girl rode down a broken trail on the side of one of the lower Sierras. By her side walked a tall man with quick, keen eyes. When they broke from the edge of the forest, she checked her horse, and they stood looking down on the upper valley of the Feather River.

Far away the water burned jewel bright under the sun, and almost directly below them were the green and red roofs of a small village. Here the trail forked — one branch winding west along the mountainside and the other dropping straight down toward the village.

"Which way shall it be?" she asked. "I don't know where the west trail leads, but this straight one takes us down to the village, and that means the law."

"Jerry," he answered, "I've been thinkin' it over, an' it seems to me that it'd be almighty hard to raise kids right above the law. Let's take the trail for the village."

ONE MAN POSSE
A Sleeper Story

"One Man Posse" appeared in the premier issue of Popular Publications' short-lived pulp magazine, *Mavericks*, dated September, 1934. It was one of five stories Faust wrote about a hero named Sleeper. This character had many similarities to Faust's popular series character, Reata, whose stories had begun appearing in Street & Smith's Western Story Magazine the previous year. Both were loners, temporarily beholden to a peddler — in both cases known as Pop — and, while neither carried a gun, both were adept in outsmarting the most vicious of adversaries — Sleeper with a knife and Reata with a rope. In "One Man Posse" Sleeper is assigned to go up against the infamous outlaw Charlie Loder by Pop Lowry. The reader also learns how Sleeper comes by his loyal horse, Careless. "Inverness" and "Death in Alkali Flat" — two of the other Sleeper stories — can be found in MORE TALES OF THE WILD WEST (Circle® Westerns, 1999).

CHAPTER
ONE

"A Horse Ain't A Bloodhound"

Pop Lowry blinked his faded eyes at the first shaft of the early June sun. He came to life at once, his lank, spare frame seeming to gather itself upward in layers from the tarp spread out on the grassy slope near the cluster of black rocks. His dressing was simple — merely putting on his coat and pulling on a pair of down-at-the-heel cowhide boots.

But there was something wrong with the left boot. Pop swore, pulled it off, and squinted inside, his gnarled fingers exploring the insole. Then he grunted, replaced the inner sole, and tugged on the footgear again. It was only then he remembered to look about, down the slope, past where his three mules were tethered. He did not turn around in time to see a dark shadow sink into nothingness on top of the nearest black rock. Had he done so, he might have made even more haste in saddling and loading the mules.

For Pop, who lived in secret fear of being robbed of the peddler's stock which he packed by muleback over a thousand mile route, had gotten a warning at the last ranch he had visited. Wild Bill Belling was rumored to be hiding out somewhere in this territory. Wild Bill, rustler, killer and all-round bad *hombre*, had been the lieutenant of the notorious Charlie Loder, and had made a successful getaway when a determined crowd of possemen had corralled Loder and taken him to jail. If Belling had known — as he well might, through the rustling of the leaves — that Pop Lowry had been instrumental in getting a reward placed on his head . . . the old peddler's eyes narrowed in anxiety as he passed the heel of his hand over his sweat-beaded forehead.

Abruptly he stooped and seemed to search anxiously through the short grass at his feet. Twice he straightened, twice again he searched, muttering to himself, looking more than ever like some skinny, wizened creature of the wasteland who would scuttle back into hiding at the first sign of human approach.

Presently a voice, coming from behind and above him, drawled: "It's in the crack of that rock, yonder."

Pop Lowry straightened with a jerk and looked wildly about. He saw nothing at first, then made out, reclining on top of the largest black rock, a tanned youngster in his early twenties — a fellow in ragged and sun-bleached Levi's, who wore a limp-brimmed colorless hat on his head and homemade moccasins on his feet.

"Sleeper!" exclaimed the startled Lowry with relief. "How long you been here?"

The question was rhetorical; Pop Lowry knew he could scarcely expect an answer, for the kid — the stray, maybe half-locoed kid called Sleeper — would talk only when he chose. Pop Lowry frowned, troubled wrinkles forming between his beetling gray brows. He fished from his pocket a square of cut-plug and put a certain venom into the strength with which he bit off a corner of the plug. Then he went over to the flat rock and peered into the crack that seamed its surface. From the crack he lifted a long blacksnake whip. He sleeked the lash through his gnarled fingers, while he turned to the ragged kid.

Sleeper — "ear-notched, but mostly maverick," men said of him — had stretched himself flat on the rock with his hands under his head and let the sun beat fully on his face.

"How'd you know I was lookin' for that blacksnake?" asked Pop querulously.

"You couldn't be lookin' for anything else," drawled the kid. "That's the only thing you didn't have. An' it had to be in that crack, 'cause the grass is too short to hide anything from eyes like yours." He yawned again.

Sleeper's blue-black hair might have been either Irish or Indian, but the deep, sea-blue of his eyes gave the former race predominance in him. As he lay there, stretched out languidly, his suppleness of body suggested infinite speed of foot and hand, which had come to him from living most of his life under the roof of the sky. No one knew what happened to him in the winter; everyone — cattlemen, townspeople, miners, nesters — knew that he would appear with the first of the warm weather, when the bunch grass and blue-joint began to get green in the bottomlands.

Sleeper said drowsily: "I wanted to talk to you about something, Pop. Talk about money."

The peddler spat on the grass and left a small brown stain upon it. He snorted. "Money! Huh! You ain't got use for money. I always thought you lazied around, eatin' the wind you could raise. *You* don't need money."

"A thousand dollars is more than money," Sleeper said softly. "It . . . it's a chance, a thousand dollars is . . ."

"What thousand?"

"The *dinero* you offered for the capture of that outlaw, Belling."

Lowry snorted again. "Ah-h. I didn't offer no reward for Belling. A lot of ranchers along my route, they been talking to me, saying this Belling's been raisin' hell with their herds, even killed a couple of folks, they said. I said why didn't they get together and ante up a reward for him. Then maybe fellers would be more interested in riskin' their lives, tryin' to get him. That would put an end to his hellin' around."

"I got a pretty good idea how to get him. I aim to get that thousand dollars. Pop."

"You do, eh?" the peddler smiled expansively. He could well afford to take a little time to fool with Sleeper. Besides — maybe the kid might have some ideas. Sleeper got around in all sorts of strange places where a normal man might hole up. "Well, then, if you're so smart, just how'd you go about trackin' him?"

Sleeper's blue eyes blinked as he scratched his head. "Why, they say his horse was caught a few days ago down near Plummett. This Belling's a powerful big man, and that horse was maybe the best friend he had.

He can't ride just any horse that happens to come along. I'd turn his horse loose and track it. Maybe it would lead to some of Belling's hideouts. A feller could do it easy, if he knew that horse, marked the shape of its hoofprints, and the length of its walking step and its trot and its canter and its gallop. Belling'd be asleep, and then . . ."

"Hell!" crowed the peddler. "Belling'd wake up an' jump right on that horse. By the time any man had a chance to take a shot at him, Belling'd be long gone. I never heard any such crazy notion. You think a horse is a bloodhound?"

"That's what I do," said Sleeper, and he relaxed more completely than ever in the sun.

Lowry moved to get into the saddle. "Yah! You mean you'd've daydreamed till it would have seemed like you'd done it . . . but you wouldn't dare to come within ten miles of a killer like Belling." He put one foot into the stirrup.

"It *was* sort of scary," agreed Sleeper. "But I got him. That's why I wanted to see you about the thousand dollars."

"You got him where?" shouted Lowry.

"Over there in a buggy," said Sleeper. He sat up and pointed. "Right there on the trail."

Lowry leaped around the corner of the rock and saw a ramshackle old buggy, each of whose wheels leaned in a different direction. A big man was lashed into the seat beside the driver's place, a big man without a hat and with flaming red hair that stood up on end as though in a wind. Lowry noted he was so securely tied, he had given up struggling with the rawhide thongs that bound him.

"Belling!" yelled Lowry, and started on a run toward the buggy.

"Get up, Pokey!" called Sleeper.

The mule, which was harnessed between the shafts, at once struck out on a brisk trot.

"Hey! Whoa! Whoa, mule! Whoa, you fool!" shouted Lowry.

"Pokey won't stop for anybody but me," said Sleeper.

"Damn it!" cried Lowry. "Stop the fool mule before it runs over the edge of the cliff!"

"Whoa, boy," called Sleeper, and the mule stopped. "So what about the thousand dollars?" yawned Sleeper.

"Thousand dollars? You don't expect me to carry that much around with me, do you?" asked Lowry in a complaining voice.

"Just give me your left boot, and that will do," answered Sleeper.

Pop Lowry started so violently that his feet almost left the ground. He looked down at his left boot.

"I'd as soon have what's under the insole of that boot as any thousand dollars," said Sleeper.

"Kid," growled the peddler, "you know too dog-gone much."

"Money makes a feller want to scratch," said Sleeper. "And your foot itched when you shoved it into that boot a while ago."

Lowry stared for a moment. Then he pulled off his boot, took the insole out of it, and produced several rumpled greenbacks. He drew on the boot again, and advanced toward Sleeper.

Sleeper pulled out a heavy, bone-handled hunting knife and began to spin it high in the air. When it came down, he caught it on the top of the thumbnail, making it land on the point and stand straight up.

"Great thunder!" gasped Lowry. "Where'd you learn that trick?"

"Easy," said Sleeper. "It just takes time to learn, and I've got plenty of time. You jerk your hand down as the point of the knife hits the nail, and the point hardly makes a scratch."

"Suppose you don't move your hand fast enough, your thumb is split through the end?"

"Yeah. But you want to move your hand fast enough."

The peddler held out the money in his left hand. With the left hand, Sleeper accepted it; in his right hand he held the long knife, so sharp that the light seemed to be dripping off the point.

Lowry looked at that sleepily smiling, tanned face, and then glanced at the knife. "You're a thousand dollars richer than I ever expected to see you, kid. But you done a mighty good job," said Lowry.

"It just took a little time. Thanks," said Sleeper. He stood up on the edge of the rock and jumped. It was ten feet to the ground below, but he landed on legs that flexed as such perfect springs that the brim of his tattered hat hardly flopped with the shock. He stepped to the buggy, and, pulling on the knot-end of the lariat that bound Belling, he set the big man free.

Belling, shaking the bonds from his body, leaped out of the buggy with a roar. But the rope had gripped his big muscles until they were numb. He staggered and almost fell.

Then Lowry's calm voice said: "Steady, Belling. I wanna talk to you a bit before I take you to jail." An enormous, old-fashioned hogleg was in his fist.

The red-headed outlaw turned toward the peddler with a scowl. "You bought me, did you? I'm gonna see you in hell for this," he declared.

Sleeper was already in the driver's place; Pokey broke into a trot.

"Hey, wait. Hey, Sleeper!" shouted the peddler.

But Sleeper rattled down the trail in the old buggy without seeming to hear the shouts.

CHAPTER
TWO

"The Golden Stallion"

Sleeper leaned against the fence that surrounded the big corral. Inside, a golden chestnut stallion was being led back and forth. The kid had in one hand a piece of soft white pine; with the other hand he used a knife, drawing from the pine stick shavings so thin that they curled up like wood before a sharp plane — they were so thin that the sun shone through them as easily as through ice. Sleeper gave great care to his whittling. He usually paid much attention to small things.

He was so absorbed that he appeared to be paying little attention to the words of the men around him, although the entire town of White Water had turned out to attend the sale of Careless. There was reason for the excitement. In the first place, the big stallion, Careless, was the finest horse that White Water had ever seen. In the second place, it was known that this horse had been the favorite mount of Charlie Loder, that vaunted bandit who was now serving a twenty-five year term in prison, so far as anyone knew. In the third place, it was equally well known that the possession of the horse had descended to that brutal former partner of Loder — Wild Bill Belling. And fourthly, and perhaps it was this that

105

had brought interest to a fever pitch, Careless had been stolen out of the corral of Sheriff Bill Collins, had been absent for five days, and then had been returned, in perfect condition, and in the middle of the night, to that same corral.

Sleeper, who could have told something about the stealing and the return of the stallion, raised his head as he heard a man near him say: "Whoever buys Careless ain't gonna have him long. Not with Charlie Loder on the trail again."

That made Sleeper say: "Is Charlie Loder on the trail again?"

The tall cowboy who had just spoken turned and glanced with a familiar contempt at Sleeper. He surveyed him from his tattered hat to his clumsy-looking moccasins.

"Don't you know nothing, Sleeper?" he asked. "Ain't you heard that Loder busted loose out of prison last week?"

"He don't hear nothin', and, if he did, he couldn't savvy it," laughed the companion of the tall cowpuncher.

Sleeper paid no heed. As for the opinions of his fellows, they never troubled him a great deal. How to get the next meal with the least outlay of effort was his daily problem. What other men said and felt mattered less than nothing to him.

Here he heard Sheriff Bill Collins saying loudly: "There's room up there in front for you, Mister Williams. Yes, sir . . . there's room up in front for you no matter what's happenin' in White Water."

106

Sleeper drew the thinnest of the shavings from the face of the glistening bit of pine. He saw the rich rancher, Henry Williams, ride through the crowd with the sheriff beside him. At the shoulder of the rancher appeared his daughter, Kate. She was the beauty of White Water. She had a way of looking straight ahead of her and smiling, when other people were near. Pretty girls are like that. They adopt the pose that shows them to the best advantage while they appear unconscious of what is going on, and all the admiration which is pouring toward them.

Here a sudden burst of neighing made Sleeper turn. He saw Careless pull back on the lead rope and heard him trumpet a call for freedom.

Sleeper whistled, a thin, sharp note, not overloud, and the golden stallion at once stopped his neigh, stopped his resistance. He turned his lordly head toward the kid who said: "Steady, boy!"

Careless nickered a soft note of recognition and submitted to the handling of the man who was leading him.

"Where'd *you* git to know Careless?" demanded the tall cowpuncher.

"We've had some talks together," answered Sleeper quietly.

"He can talk horse-talk better than man-talk, maybe?" suggested the cowboy's companion.

"He maybe can talk horse-talk," said the tall cowboy, "but he ain't got horse sense."

There was a loud laugh at this, but Sleeper was again deep in the problems of his whittling. He seemed to pay no heed. Not a trace of color appeared in his face, nor did he appear as if he had heard the affront. A nameless fellow, fatherless, motherless, vagrant, indolent, worthless — why should he be proud?

A moment later, he had his shoulder flicked by the end of a quirt.

It was the sheriff, bawling out: "Sleeper, what you doing there in a front seat? Get out and let your superiors have a show, will you? Here's Mister Williams . . . and his daughter need a place close to the fence. Move back and let them step in!"

"No, Sheriff," protested the clear, quick voice of the girl. "We don't want to displace anyone."

"You ain't displacing anybody, when you displace Sleeper," said the sheriff. "He ain't even got a name. So how could you be displacing anything?"

Sleeper did not protest. He retreated smoothly through the crowd and allowed rich Mr. Williams to take that coveted place near the fence, with his daughter before him. She turned her brown eyes anxiously toward Sleeper, and her lips said silently: "Sorry." Her eyes said — "Sorry." — also. But Sleeper paid no heed.

He drifted back through the crowd after the sheriff's horse, and, as big Bill Collins reached the outskirts of the crowd, Sleeper rapped his knuckles on the taps of the McClellan stirrups.

"Yeah . . . yeah?" snapped Collins, looking down. Then he softened. "Oh, it's you, is it? Well, kid, I just wanted your place at the fence for Mister Williams. I didn't want to drag you out of the crowd."

Sleeper, with an odd, fixed smile, looked up at the sheriff. "You remembered me today, Sheriff," he said. "I'll be remembering you tomorrow."

"Hey? What do you mean, you fool?" demanded the sheriff with a frown.

Sleeper's smile persisted. It was open-eyed, steady; it made cold chills crawl for no reason in particular, up the sheriff's spine. He was angered and a little ashamed because he felt this reaction, and he didn't know why.

"I wanna tell you something, kid," he said. "I got a mind to run you out of this town, anyway. We don't want vagrants around here, we don't want know-nothin's nor do-nothin's."

But Sleeper was already drifting away.

He heard a voice call: "Here's where you get your genu-wine silver saddle fittings, gents. Mexican silver *conchos*, inlaid bits and buckles. Here's where you get 'em, at the cheapest price. Anybody want any more?"

It was the peddler, Pop Lowry, his nasal voice ringing through the noise of the crowd. His appearance was a little unusual, for his hat was worn crookedly to accommodate a thick white bandage that was wound about his head.

Sleeper paused and stared at him.

"Why, hello, Sleeper," said the peddler. "I been wanting to see you." He tossed his trinkets into the mule's *alforjas* and stepped closer to Sleeper.

"Hello, Pop," said Sleeper. "Did Belling get away?"

"You'd think I'd leave him get away?" growled Lowry.

"How would I know? You weren't paying a thousand dollars just to put him in jail, were you?" Sleeper's voice was ironic.

Lowry blinked. "You're loco . . . always been loco, Sleeper." And then, in a lower voice: "How many people you told about catching Belling, kid?"

"Why should I tell anybody?" asked Sleeper.

"Why? Why should you tell . . . after the way you captured Belling? Son, everybody in town must of heard you crow by the time I got down here."

"Was that why you put on the bandage, Pop?" asked Sleeper without a smile.

"I dunno what you're talking about," the peddler growled.

"Just to show how hard you fought to keep him, when he took you by surprise. Didn't he take you by surprise?"

"He sure did!" agreed Pop Lowry fervently. Then he added in a softer growl: "Just what you mean?"

"That he took you by surprise. Socked you right over the head and left you for dead. Isn't that what happened?"

Lowry moistened his wide, thin lips. "You're a queer kid," he observed.

"It's a queer world," agreed Sleeper. "That's why queer people fit into it so well."

Pop Lowry chewed on some cut-plug. "I wanna talk to you," he said. His teeth clicked through the plug of tobacco.

"Here I am."

"You . . . you mean you haven't told a soul about catching . . . him?"

"No. You damn' fool, would that double my income?"

"Sleeper, stop whittling and listen here. You got parts, somehow. You got quality, maybe. The rest of these boggleheads, they can't see it. But for years I been waiting for you to grow up . . . and that time has come."

"You want me to catch Belling again, for Lord's sake?" smiled Sleeper.

"I want . . . listen to me . . . somebody's going to bid plenty *dinero* to get this horse, Careless."

"Maybe you're right," conceded Sleeper. "Whoever gets him . . . *if* he gets him," he added grimly.

"Whoever gets that horse is going to lead him away. And the man that leads Careless away is going to meet Belling and turn the horse over to him. I know . . . never mind how I know. And then Belling is going to ride on until he meets another man, and then the two of them are going to ride to Chimney Creek."

"Then you could get some head-money at Chimney Creek, if you wait for the pair of them there, and if you had the . . . guts, eh?" suggested Sleeper. "There's a price on Belling now, even without *your* thousand."

"Wait a minute, son, I'm going to trust you. The thing is this . . . maybe Belling *won't* ride with the other man to Chimney Creek. Understand? And wherever Belling goes, I want you to follow him . . . and, when you've got where he hides out with the other man, I want you to ride back and tell me. I'm going to

111

be in the old shack east of White Water. You know . . .
where Ike Matthews used to live."

"I know. And I bring you back to the two of them, I
suppose?"

"Yeah. You got it. You bring me back to the two of
them." The peddler's eyes turned into bright slits.

"What's the price?"

"I'll give you five days' wages . . . ten dollars. No, by
God, I'll make it twenty!"

Sleeper smiled. "I've got a new price. I've turned
bounty hunter," he said. "Just exactly one thousand
dollars."

"Oh, God!" intoned the peddler. "You think I'm
made of money? You gone loco?"

"Maybe you had another bill in your boots,"
suggested Sleeper. "Or if you didn't, find somebody
else who can trail Careless."

The peddler pulled off his hat and wiped his bald
head with the flat of his hand. "Well," he said, "I
dunno. I'll pay you a thousand dollars spot cash for the
job . . . and damn you, Sleeper, for askin' that much."

"I risk my head, and you risk a few pennies," said
Sleeper cheerfully, "but maybe your man *won't* lead
Careless away."

"I'm telling you what'll happen. Don't ask fool
questions," answered Pop Lowry.

Sleeper's eyes narrowed the least bit. "Tell me
another thing. Before Charlie Loder went to jail . . . ?"

The peddler started violently. He took a step closer
to Sleeper. "Who put Loder's name into this game?" he
demanded.

112

"I did," said Sleeper. "I'm asking you . . . before Charlie Loder went to prison, wasn't he running around with Kate Williams?"

"Huh?" gasped the peddler. "What the hell difference does that make?"

Sleeper said nothing. He just grinned.

"Well," explained the peddler, "he was running around with her, yeah, you could call it that. Why not? Best-looking man and the best-looking girl? Why shouldn't they go together?"

"Of course, they should," agreed Sleeper.

"Well . . . keep your mouth shut . . . maybe I'll be useful to you," Pop Lowry said.

At that moment the voice of the auctioneer began to bawl: "Ready, gents . . . loosen up your pants pockets . . . trot out your hard cash. We're sellin' the finest horse that ever went under the hammer, boys! From barrel to hocks, he's a real man's horse . . . he's had to be, 'cause he's been grain-fed without a bit of hay. The owners of this horse have had to travel far and fast and never bothered about a bill of sale. Look at him, gents . . . see that sleek arch . . . the shape of that head . . . you can't afford to miss this one chance! Gents," — and with a look at Kate Williams — "ladies, I'm askin' for an opening bid . . . on Careless!"

"Two hundred and fifty dollars," came an excited yell. And with that offer there was a loud burst of derisive laughter.

CHAPTER
THREE

"Sleeper Plays His Hand"

The bid seemed foolish enough, considering the quality of the stallion that was still pacing up and down the corral. Now he threw up his head and neighed again. He was like leaf gold — and he burned in the sunlight. But still, two hundred and fifty dollars was a good deal of money for a horse in a community which knew that a good cow pony could be bought for fifty. For a hundred and fifty dollars, one could get a trained cutting horse that would follow a calf through a herd of cows and, turning short, would work almost faster than the thought of an ordinary rider. Two hundred and fifty dollars was a good deal — and yet, there stood that great golden stallion!

As the neighing died out, a man called to the auctioneer: "He's laughin' at you, Jerry!"

"Two hundred and fifty dollars," shouted the auctioneer, "offered by Mister Jeremiah Bangor . . . thank you, Jerry . . . thank you for starting the dance, but I reckon that nobody ain't gonna walk off with Careless with a price like that. Careless is his name . . . careless have been the gents that have rode him, and careless he is by nature. Sheriff Collins, you've wore out

114

a pile of good horseflesh, tryin' to follow this Careless. You can tell 'em can he run."

"Three hundred!" said the voice. And then it went up to five hundred. It was a lot of money, when you could hire a good cowhand for forty a month and beans. Suppose that a man were careful and saved twenty a month — five hundred meant the savings of two years. Five hundred for a bit of horseflesh enclosed within a single skin.

There was a pause. Then, suddenly a voice said: "And ten!"

"Shorty Joe Bennett," murmured someone. "Shorty Joe must be diggin' down to the toe of the sock. Is he drunk?"

Shorty Joe Bennett stood on the lowest bar of the corral fence. He blinked as all eyes turned upon him, and his face turned a deep red. But he kept his grip on the top rail of the fence with those tense, white-knuckled hands, and with his eyes he kept his hold on the burning beauty of the stallion.

"Five hundred and ten dollars bid by Shorty Joe Bennett!" shouted the auctioneer. "Good work, Joe! Come on, boys! Everybody's in this. Careless is worth any man's entire spread. Five hundred is plenty, but he's worth more than that. There's a horse that nobody will catch you on!"

A girl's voice cried: "Fifty!"

"Five hundred and fifty offered by Miss Kate Williams!" called the auctioneer. There was applause. The girl's blue eyes were shining. What a picture she would make on the back of that stallion!

The sheriff himself roared out: "Six hundred!" His face was swollen. He pulled at his soft, tieless collar to give himself better breathing.

"*And* ten!" droned the voice of Shorty Joe Bennett.

The sheriff flung both arms into the air. "By God, I offered all I could!" he cried. Tears were in his eyes.

"Six-fifty!" called Kate Williams pleasantly, after turning to look at her father. There was a shout of enthusiasm.

"Sixty!" snapped Joe Bennett. He was an ugly man with a vast jaw and a face that sloped steadily back to the roots of his hair. He looked like an ugly overgrowth of a dwarf.

There was a silence. Kate Williams turned to her father. There was a brief colloquy between them, the rancher shaking his head.

"*Six* hundred and sixty dollars offered for this glorious stallion!" cried the auctioneer. "Do I hear an up?"

"Seven hundred!" cried the voice of Kate Williams.

At this, a cheer was raised.

"*And* ten," said the dour Joe Bennett. Silence followed. It was a gross insult even to think of such a fellow as Bennett on the back of the great chestnut.

Then another voice said, so quietly that it was hardly heard: "Eight hundred dollars!"

All heads snapped around. "Sleeper, d'you mean that you're biddin' . . . or are you jokin'?" asked the auctioneer.

There was a roar of laughter. The town lazy man, the nameless tramp, the idler Sleeper, bidding eight hundred dollars?

116

For answer, Sleeper held up a stiff sheaf of greenbacks in his left hand. And the laughter was wiped from every face. A little lane opened before Sleeper, and he advanced from the rear of the crowd to the fence.

"And ten!" snarled Joe Bennett.

It was getting to be a lot of money.

People could see Kate Williams pleading with her father, but this time his shake of the head was obdurate and final.

"Nine hundred!" cried Sleeper loudly.

And now a sudden yell went up from the throats of the audience. They had become, all of them, mere spectators. Even the daughter of the wealthy rancher was out of it; you might say that all sensible men were out of it — in a land where a very good nag could be bought for fifty dollars. There remained two fanatics who loved a horse more than they loved money. One of them was the deformed Joe Bennett. The other was the town tramp, in rags. People gripped each other by the arm, and stared, and waited with hungry ears.

"Mister Sleeper!" yelled the auctioneer, giving the name a title because of the new respect which suddenly was filling his breast. "Did I hear you say nine hundred dollars?"

Sleeper, from his pocket, added another bill to the sheaf in his left, raised hand.

"Yes," he said. "Nine hundred dollars."

Now a very strange thing happened, for the great stallion, hearing this voice, whirled suddenly, snatched the lead rope out of the hand of the man controlling

117

him, and rushed for the fence, at the spot where Sleeper stood.

There, people shrank back, thinking that the great monster would leap the bars. Instead, he skidded to a halt, and then thrust his head between the bars and into the arms of Sleeper.

What a shout answered that demonstration from the fierce horse. Men beat one another about the shoulders. Women screamed. And into their cry dissolved the voice of Kate Williams, who stood by, with eyes that opened wide and stared into the eager face of Sleeper.

This was the idler, the worthless one, the tramp of half a dozen counties thereabouts — and now he was intent on some great, divine purpose — and God or the devil seemed to have filled his hands with money for it. But if such a fellow should offer nine hundred for a horse, why should not the rich offer all they owned?

"And ten," groaned the voice of Shorty Joe Bennett.

There was no applause. Men and women were seeing the beautiful head of the stallion caressed by the hands of the tramp, and an awe moved their spirits.

"Daddy," said the voice of Kate Williams — and it was audible in this sudden silence — "help him! Help him buy the horse!"

"Nine hundred and ten offered," said the auctioneer. He stood half-crouched, sweating, excited like a runner about to start for a race. "Do I hear an up?"

"Dad!" pleaded the voice of Kate Williams. "*Do* help Sleeper!"

118

"An infernal low tramp? A worthless idler? Help him?" exploded the rancher. "I'll see him damned first!"

And everyone heard that.

Sleeper, standing close by with one hand stroking the head of Careless, turned a little and took off his tattered hat and bowed to the girl with the grace of the blood, not of teaching. "I have to have him with my own money . . . not with gifts," he said. Turning back toward the auctioneer, he cried loudly: "One thousand dollars!"

Pandemonium followed. Men were climbing the rails to see better. They saw, among other things, that Sleeper had added another bill to the sheaf which he held in his left hand.

The cheering, the wild yelling lasted for some time, but as it died down, the inevitable voice of Shorty Joe Bennett growled: "*And* ten!"

The auctioneer cried through the deadly silence: "A thousand and ten dollars offered for Careless. People that understand would offer two thousand, three thousand. Gentlemen, remember yourselves!" He looked at the rich rancher Williams, as he said this.

The girl, people saw, was staring toward Sleeper, the tramp. Then they saw that Sleeper's head had fallen in utter defeat.

"Going for a thousand and ten dollars!" cried the auctioneer. "Going to Shorty Bennett for a thousand and ten dollars . . . do I hear an up?"

That same tall cowpuncher who had mocked at Sleeper before exclaimed: "I got forty dollars, Sleeper, and it's yours. Give him an up, kid!"

"I won't buy him with borrowed money," said Sleeper. He lifted his head and nodded: "Thanks, old-timer."

People were more stunned by this, perhaps, than by all the strange performance which had gone before.

"Going!" yelled the auctioneer, waving both arms. "Going for a thousand and ten . . . going . . . going . . . think of it, gentlemen, the finest horse that ever stepped in White Water . . . for a thousand and ten . . . going . . . going . . . going to Joe Bennett! Sold, Joe! Shorty, Careless belongs to you."

But Careless was paying no attention to this. He was trying, with his prehensile upper lip, to get into the coat pocket of Sleeper, and Sleeper, with deeply bowed head, was stroking him vaguely across the forehead.

Shorty Joe marched across the ring and grabbed the lead rope of Careless and drew him away.

Sleeper, gripping the rail of the fence, made no move until he heard the voice of the girl say: "I'm sorry, Sleeper. I'm terribly sorry. You loved him. I can see that."

He lifted his eyes and saw her through a haze which told him that he was looking through tears. But what amazed him was to see that tears were openly in her own eyes.

"Here, Kate, here," said her father, taking her by the arm. "All damned nonsense! If he has a thousand, where did he get it?"

"By risking my neck to get it," answered Sleeper. There were other men who heard him say this, and they were willing to retell it in the barroom afterward. "Did you ever get a penny of your money the same way, Mister Williams?"

But Williams made no answer. He hurriedly took his daughter through the crowd.

CHAPTER
FOUR

"A Bullet In The Back"

Sleeper could have remained in White Water and drunk away days and days at the expense of other men, because, by this effort, he had become suddenly a sort of minor hero. In a country where all men loved horses, he, the tramp, had proven that he loved a horse better than the rest. In a subtle way, he had shamed the great Henry C. Williams by offering up his skin, whereas Williams would not give even the price of a few of his thousands of fat steers.

Two people emerged from this with credit — Kate Williams and Sleeper. And Shorty Joe Bennett emerged with the stallion, but with the suspicion of the crowd attached to him. For Shorty, all his life, had never done anything better than cheat at cards.

Sleeper, working his way through the crowd, avoided the hearty invitations that poured in on him. He found the peddler walking at his side, saying: "What's the matter, kid? Would you give every penny to get a horse? Better have some place to go before you buy the way of getting there."

Sleeper, looking him in the eye, answered: "You're a crook, Pop. I've always known that you were a crook.

Today, I'm sure of it. But I'm damned, if I care how much of a crook you are, so long as I can get Careless."

He expected a curse in response. He was amazed to hear the peddler say: "Well, well, well! It's always with a fellow like you that I do the biggest business. Sleeper, I thought you was worth your price before. But now I'll pay you two thousand, if you bring me to Belling and his partner . . . any place in Chimney Creek Cañon!"

Sleeper seemed not to hear him, and walked hastily away.

Through the late afternoon, through the twilight, Shorty Joe Bennett led the stallion by devious paths and buried trails across the hills. Many a time he stopped and looked back, and each time he did so, a form sank to the ground behind a rock or glided behind a tree to shelter.

Then, in a deep, dark hollow, Sleeper saw his man greeted by a rider who paused only a moment, took the reins of the stallion, and went on.

After that, it was hard work — very hard. To follow a trotting horse on foot requires the best muscle and the best wind of a well-trained athlete. But Sleeper was well-trained. Those endless wanderings of his through the hills had given him a body of tough fibers. He was a creature of whalebone and fire. Now he added to his strength all the power of his soul. For he was on the trail of the one thing in the world that he wanted — the golden stallion, Careless.

Darkness came. Part of the time he ran by his knowledge of the land, sighting toward this gap in the hills or that forested ravine. But again, where there were several courses to choose from, he would crawl on hands and knees, lighting matches, until he found again the print of hoofs which were as well known to him as human faces to ordinary eyes.

That was how he covered the difficult corners of his assignment. He was thinking little of the two thousand dollars that had been promised to him by the strange peddler. He was thinking of Careless only, and how the great stallion had come to his voice.

With a groaning eagerness, he stuck to the trail, still running when his lungs were on fire, when his knees failed him, when his head was pulled over on one shoulder by the immensity of his exertion. Often, as he passed some running water, he wanted to throw himself headlong into the little stream and cool the heat of his blood. But he dared not waste even an instant. Otherwise, perhaps, he would have missed the spectacle, by starlight, of two riders, not one, lifting against the horizon.

Two — not one. The words of the peddler had come true. Big red-headed Belling had led the golden stallion and had given him to a companion.

Who could that man be? Who had placed the money for the purchase in the hands of Shorty Joe Bennett? Who was there whom Belling feared or loved enough, in all this world, to force him to give up Careless? What was the interest and what was the information of the peddler? Where were these two riders bound? Certainly, they were not headed for Chimney Creek. To what

124

point, then? And how was he to get back to the old shack east of White Water in order to warn Pop?

No, he was first to run the pair to ground. He, with his unaided legs, and the pair of them on fine horses. Why was it that Pop Lowry wanted them to go to Chimney Creek?

These questions he repeated to himself over and over again in a sort of hypnotic dream, his brain going weary with the words. And then he heard the thunders of the cataracts of White Water Creek and dipped into the great, dark ravine through which the creek plowed its way.

He ran as fast as he could, but his knees were gone. There was no spring in his ankles. He had to swing his leaden, nerveless legs from the hips, and use his will power to make every stride. Then he saw, like an eye opening through the darkness, a single ray of light. He stopped. The light had disappeared as though it had been one ray shot from a dark lantern. He pushed through a hedge of tall brush close beside the rushing of White Water Creek and saw the ray of light again. Going ahead carefully, he made out at last the lines of a cabin almost over-clouded by a great growth of trees. Still closer, he came on the dim silhouettes of two horses, and even the blanket of the night could not altogether hide the gleam of the silken coat of Careless.

A faint whicker of recognition came from the big horse. Sleeper stood close, his arm around the neck of the stallion, and listened to a muttering of voices inside the cabin. But he could not make out the words because of the roar of the cataracts, which were only a little way down the creek, filled the air with a burden of sound.

He stood back from the cabin, and the stallion tried to follow but was pushed away. At those pushing hands, Careless sniffed curiously and nipped very gently Sleeper's sleeve.

But Sleeper was watching a spot of dull light that broke through the roof and painted a round of faint silver on the foliage of a tree overhead. A moment later, like a cat, he was climbing the log wall, then stretching himself up the slant of the roof. It was the flimsiest sort of an affair of thatch and cross-branches. It had not been patched for years, and it gave with a slight sagging and shuddering under Sleeper's weight. But he continued until he was able to look down through the hole in the thatch at what was happening below. There he saw Belling, digging vigorously with a rusty spade by lantern light. He was opening a hole in the earthen floor of the shack.

By Belling's side a tall fellow walked up and down, a man with a handsome face full of command. He was not more than thirty. He had the clean-cut quality of a youth and the strength of maturity about him. His face was that of Charlie Loder. Sleeper remained at his post with a slight chill running through his blood. He would have felt the same emotion, if he had come on a sleek-sided panther, facing him in a lonely, narrow mountain trail.

"Belling," said Loder, "how many times have your hands itched to come up here and dig the stuff out?"

"Fifty times," said Belling, chuckling. "But every time I got the itch, I remembered that no jail would hold you long, Charlie. So I just swallowed and held hard."

"This peddler . . . old Pop Lowry," said Loder. "You say that he knows there's loot somewhere in the hills?"

"He's got his trap set over in Chimney Creek," answered Belling, laughing again. "He had me in a hole, and I had to talk up. I said all I knew was that the stuff was in Chimney Creek, but that you were the only one that knew the exact spot. So I suppose he's got half a dozen thugs over there waiting for us. Him and me are to split two ways."

"Belling," said Loder, "either you're pretty square, or you're damned afraid of me."

"Wasn't I right?" demanded Belling. "*Did* the jail hold you?"

Loder laughed.

"But salting down that guard . . . that won't do you any good with the Williams girl," said Belling, driving the old shovel deep into the ground.

"She's so crazy about me," said Loder, "that it won't make any difference. Desperate man, struggling for his rights of freedom . . . you know. She'll be sorrier than ever for me."

"You mean she thinks you got clean hands all the way through?"

"That's what I mean," chuckled Loder. "There's no fool like a female fool."

"But how you gonna work the marriage gag, when you're already married?"

"Leave that to me, feller. I'll show her a gent who looks like a minister, and I'll put a real gold ring on her finger. After that . . . her old man can buy her way out. That's all I ever had my eye on . . . his coin. And he's got plenty of it."

"She's a pretty kid," said Belling.

"Yeah? She doesn't interest me," declared Loder. "Too damn sweet and clean. The trouble with a girl like that, she's got no background. She don't mean anything. She don't understand."

"No?" queried Belling.

"No. She don't understand. She won't smoke . . . she won't sit down and have a drink with you. How you going to spend time with a girl like that? And I've always got to be watching my tongue, when I'm with her. One crack and I'd be ruined."

"She's sure loco about you."

"Because she thinks that poor Charlie Loder has had so much bad luck. That's the reason. The world has used poor Charlie so badly that she's going to make everything up to him. She believes in me the way an Irishman believes in any lost cause."

Here the shovel of Belling grated on metal, and Loder suddenly leaned over the hole in the ground. The top of a large tin was now exposed, and Belling drew a five gallon oil can out of the earth.

"Here it is, chief!" he exclaimed.

"Open it up!" snapped Loder.

It was accordingly opened by Belling, who first took out a flat package wrapped in oiled silk.

"You remember! That's you and Myrtle."

128

"That's right," said Loder. "I was all sure stampeded by Myrtle in those days. Damn her! I wouldn't be caught with her picture on me, and that's why we buried it with the coin."

"She still crazy about you?" asked Belling.

"No girl is crazy about a man after she marries him," said Loder bitterly. "She's been running around with a dance-hall dude for the last six months, and she won't get a divorce because still thinks that she can mine some dough out of me. She's out for the money, is Myrtle. Let me have a look."

He opened the package and drew out a photograph of a woman in a bridal veil. Dimly, from his spying place, Sleeper could make out the sweep of the white garment.

"There was a girl, anyway," said Loder. "Crooked . . . sure. The morals of a field mouse. But you could have a good time with her. She'd stake her last *peso* on the cards. Drink anything with a kick in it. Smoke anything that burned. I'm sort of sorry about Myrtle. And I had to bury her face along with the cash, did I? Listen, Belling . . . a year ago I was a lot younger. I was sort of a sentimental fool then."

"You sort of liked her," answered Belling. "My God, I hope none of this stuff has gone and molded on us."

"It'd be bad luck for you, if any of it was gone," said the voice of Loder, suddenly turned to iron.

Belling, stopping in his work of unwrapping the treasure, looked up anxiously at his chief. "Yeah, you'd kill me, I guess," he said thoughtfully.

"Come out of it!" commanded Loder. "I know you're straight. You're the only man in the world that I'd trust, Belling."

It was finished after several wrappings of tarpaulin had been untied. And under the eye of Sleeper lay several neat stacks of greenbacks. Pressure and earth-damp had compacted them a little and rounded the stacks at the corners.

"You wouldn't think that a hundred and ten thousand would look so small, would you?" asked Loder.

"Yeah, you wouldn't think it," said Belling. "We split it fifty-fifty?"

"Fifty-fifty?" shouted Loder.

"Hey . . . wait . . ." exclaimed Belling. "Any way you want is the way we'll split it. I thought you used to say it was an even cut?"

"Sure . . . fifty-fifty's all right," said Loder slowly.

"No. You're sour on the idea. Make it anything you want. Sixty for you and forty for me . . . seventy for you and thirty for me. Break it any way you please. You mean more than the cash to me, Charlie."

"Fifty-fifty," said Loder calmly. But there was a curiously reflective light in his eye.

Belling exclaimed: "What the devil's that?"

He had reason to look up, and so had Loder, for the whole section of the roof on which Sleeper lay had cracked and sagged, the rotten old branches yielding under the steady pressure. Vainly, Sleeper tried to slip away, down the slope of the roof; at his first movement, there was a loud crackling and rending. The whole support disappeared, and he dropped in a confusion of rotten thatch and breaking branches onto the floor of the cabin, with the yell of the two surprised men ringing in his ears.

He rebounded from the floor as swiftly as any cat and leaped for the door. He would have made it and the safety of the thick night outside, if his foot had not caught in one of the crooked boughs. He fell flat on his back and looked up into the leveled gun in the hand of Loder.

"It's Sleeper . . . it's the kid!" exclaimed Loder.

"It's the coyote that caught me and turned me over to Pop Lowry!" shouted Belling. "He's trailed me again. By God, he's got second sight or he couldn't have follered through a night like this!"

"If he's got second sight," said Loder, "maybe he can see the corner of hell that he's goin' to. Fan him, Belling."

Struggling was a folly. Sleeper did not struggle. He allowed his only weapon to be taken. It was that same long hunting knife that was almost a part of his mind, he was so expert in the use of it.

"Stand up!" snapped Loder.

Sleeper rose. Belling blocked the way to the door. He picked a length of twine from his pocket. "Slippery as a damned snake!" he commented. "When he caught me, it was like a wildcat had dropped on top of me. I couldn't do nothing."

"You mean that skinny kid handled you?" asked Loder contemptuously.

"Wait a minute," said Belling.

He tied the unresisting hands of Sleeper behind his back. Then, with a single jerk, he ripped a sleeve away.

"Look at there," he said. "Look at the twisting of them muscles over the shoulder. Look at that forearm. The harder you sock at him, the worse you get hurt. After he got my gun, I tried to mob him. I nearly busted myself in two, trying to murder him. He had me flat in a minute. And he wasn't even breathing."

"I'd like to try him," said Loder.

"Don't you do it," cautioned Belling. "Not even when his hands is tied, because his feet is hands, too. That's one thing that I found out."

"Kid," said Loder, "I'd like to try you, but I've got an appointment with a girl, and I'm late for it already. How long were you up there on the roof?"

"Just got there when the thing caved in," said Sleeper calmly.

"You're cool," said Loder. "You'll need to be icy, though, where you're going."

"Have we gotta plant off?" asked Belling.

"What you think, you fool?" demanded Loder.

"I don't think," said Belling. "He seems kind of young, is all."

"If he followed us tonight, he's a cat and can see in the dark. I don't want any cats on my trail, brother. Kid, you start for hell right now."

Sleeper set his teeth, looked at the gun, and smiled.

"Yeah, he's game," decided Loder, lowering the gun. "If he's a cat, we'll give him a chance to save one of his nine lives. We'll chuck him in the creek with his hands tied and see what he can do."

132

"With his hands tied?" exclaimed Belling. "Why, there ain't anybody, hardly, that could get out of that current even with both hands free."

"It's the only chance we'll give him," said Loder. "If you can call it a chance. Grab him and start him moving, Belling." He added: "Wait a minute." And taking the photograph of himself and his wife in its wrapping of oiled silk, he thrust it inside the breast of Sleeper's shirt. "Take this to hell with you, kid," he said. "Myrtle will be down there before long, if I have my way . . . and you can show her what I sent ahead of her. Give her my love, will you?"

He laughed, then he marched with Belling and Sleeper out into the night.

On the verge of the creek, where a high rock made the bank, they paused. The spray of the whipping currents rose as high as Sleeper's face. Down the stream he could see a streak of white that marked the commencement of the first cataract. The world was slipping away from him with the sweep of the stream.

"Shall we heave him in?" asked Belling.

"Wait a minute," answered Loder. "You show him the way."

His gun spat red, and Belling dropped to the rock, rolled over the edge of it, and spilled into the stream. Sleeper saw the sudden jerk as the current caught the body and snatched it whirling away.

"There's your fifty-fifty split!" said Loder calmly.

CHAPTER
FIVE

"Killer's Gold"

Murder seemed a small thing with the uproar of the creek in the ears and the speed of the current making a wind.

"Now, you!" said Loder, and swung the weight of his gun at the head of Sleeper. But Sleeper was already over the edge of the rock, springing out as far as he could. For his one chance in a million to live was to get himself across the creek to the farther shore. He struck the water hard, went under with his breath held, and then came to the surface, spinning out of the stream. He could swim well enough in calm water by kicking out with his legs only, but he saw now that way was totally futile. He used that moment when he was above water to send a long, shrilling whistle through the air. He had called Careless with it many a time before, and, although he knew it was vain to ask the great horse to venture into this maëlstrom, he sent out the call and his last hope with it.

Then he was underwater again. Kicking out with his legs made little difference. The stream shot him forward like a log. He had to snatch at breath like a dog at a bone in split seconds of opportunity. And he saw above

134

him a wheeling, swaying world with the thunder of the cataracts running closer to him every moment. The stone teeth of the falls would be tearing him before long.

Then he saw, running along the bank with gigantic strides and seeming to be racing through the sky, the great form of Careless. The neighing of the big horse pierced the thundering of the creek.

Careless disappeared. However great his affection for Sleeper, the stallion must have shrunk away, when he saw the leaping of the spray above White Water Creek. And Sleeper hardened his mind for the last moment of existence.

Something like a shadow fell across his mind's eye. With a new swirl of the current, he saw that it was the undaunted horse that, half lost in the smother of the stream, gained footing in the shallows of the creek and losing hoof-hold again in a moment, still struggled forward.

He was close. He was there beside Sleeper, and moving past him. A swinging stirrup clouted Sleeper's head. He snapped at it with his teeth and caught a hold which he kept with a frantic effort. Careless, neighing as though in triumph, floundered on toward the farther shore.

There was little chance for Sleeper to breathe. Most of the time his head was underwater as the currents streamed him out from the stirrup leather that sustained him. Behind him he heard the cataracts shouting louder as the water beat the stallion downstream.

When he had a chance to draw fresh breath and look up, he could see that the ears of the stallion were desperately flattened. He looked like some terrible snake-headed monster out of a primeval swamp. But there was still hope, as the farther shore drew nearer, until it seemed to Sleeper that White Water Creek gathered all its forces, lurching upward, and then whirling with a great smother of foam and spray. The stallion was picked up like so much dead wood and spun around and down the wash of the stream.

The roar of the cataracts seemed to be shouting from the skies. And then came a halt that almost jerked the teeth from the head of the Sleeper. His body streamed out on the brink of the white water. Death was there, breathing over him and calling him, but big Careless had secured foothold on the very ledge of the first cataract and once more moved toward the shore.

That firmer footing lifted him higher. In a moment he had whipped Sleeper out of the creek and through the brush on the farther bank. The jaws of Sleeper could relax their hold at last. He lay inert and had a strange sensation that the earth was receiving him and buoying him up from danger with a motherly care.

When he staggered to his feet, he could see the silhouette of a rider moving up and down the farther bank of the stream opposite the cataract, as though searching the flow of the currents for a last sight of Sleeper's body. It was not strange if he had been unable to make out that incredible rescue. Then the rider turned his horse back into the woods. He would go now, to keep that appointment for which he was late —

that meeting with Kate Williams, for what other woman would he have in mind at this time?

Sleeper, stepping back against a boulder, fumbled till he found a sharp edge of the rock and then chafed against it the cords that bound his wrists. His hands were free in a moment, free to caress the noble head of Careless, who stood dripping and trembling from his work.

Then into the wet saddle Sleeper swung himself. He put the stallion into that long striding gallop which jerked the trees away into the darkness that flowed like a river to the rear.

Loder, with over a hundred thousand dollars in his hands after that "fifty-fifty split," was going at his ease across country on the horse of his dead partner. How long would it take Sleeper to reach the old shack east of White Water Creek and give the word to Pop Lowry?

That was on the way to the Williams Ranch. There would not be time, also, to ride into White Water and raise a crowd of fighting men to head toward the ranch. Men most likely would say that the loafer was crazy, out of his head. In the meantime, Loder would be keeping his appointment with the girl, and taking her away to the unknown place where there was waiting a "fellow who looked enough like a minister to suit anybody."

Sleeper, would have to get out there and prevent the catastrophe — he, with his empty hands.

The big horse blew through the upper ravines like the wind, struck the lower valley. But the lights of White Water were far, far ahead when Sleeper turned aside down a lane that was almost overgrown with brush. He came out into a clearing where the bushes moved like waves against the moldering little shack. There was a light inside. It showed in pale streaks through the cracks between the boards.

"Lowry!" shouted Sleeper.

He swung from the back of the stallion as he spoke. The door of the shack yawned wide, and in the entrance stood the tall, bent form of the peddler. He lifted the lantern in order to throw light on the form of Sleeper, and, so doing, he illumined the gleaming baldness of his own head.

"Hello, Sleeper," said Lowry. "Damn my old eyes . . . is that Careless you got with you?"

"They didn't go to Chimney Creek," panted Sleeper.

"I know that . . . now," said Lowry. "Dog-gone me, but I listened to lies. I was takin' a long chance."

"At a hundred and ten thousand dollars, eh?" snapped Sleeper.

Lowry whistled. "As much as that?" he said. And he made a clucking sound of surprise. "Where's Belling?"

"Dead . . . murdered . . . and chewed to bits in the White Water cataracts."

The calm rejoinder of the peddler was merely: "You look kind of wet yourself, Sleeper."

"Loder killed him," said Sleeper.

"That ain't a big surprise to me. So Loder has the whole bunch of the money, now?"

"Lowry, you're not working a lone hand . . . you've got men with you . . . how many?"

"Why, I wouldn't know, exactly," said Lowry. "There's lots of good men to be hired, here and there."

"Listen . . . Loder has gone to the Williams Ranch. I'm a dead man. I mean, he thinks that I'm dead. I tell you, he has more than a hundred thousand dollars on him. Lowry, if you have ways of doing things, do them now. Can you get men to the Williams place or do I have to go into White Water and try to raise a crowd?"

"Don't raise no crowd, brother!" said Lowry. "Crowds ain't any good. For a fellow like Loder, every crowd is too dog-gone big in the mesh, and he just slips away into the brush again. I'll handle Loder . . ."

He pulled something from his pocket and blew a whistle that screamed across the night and seemed to draw a train of fire through the brain of Sleeper.

"You can have all the cash," said Sleeper. "But get there with your men, Pop. There's been murder already, tonight, and there's going to be something worse unless we're fast." He threw himself back into the saddle.

"Wait a minute! Where you going?"

"To the Williams Ranch."

"Not alone. Sleeper, listen, you fool! You'll spoil the whole idea . . ."

But Sleeper was already gone, bending low in the saddle as he shot the stallion among the trees with the branches *whishing* overhead.

He crossed the valley with big Careless running still at top speed. He passed through the gap in the hills and, coming out on the wide plateau beyond, was aware of the faint glimmering of lights ahead of him.

That was the Williams Ranch. The trembling of the lights beat into his brain like the rhythm of a galloping horse, telling him to hurry, hurry, for already it might be too late.

CHAPTER
SIX

"A Girl — And A Gun"

Even the mighty endurance of Careless was sapped before he brought his rider to the Williams ranch house. He stopped very willingly under the trees and dropped his head to wheeze for fresh breath while Sleeper made for the first light. It shone from the windows of the big living room. Long, Spanish windows, from floor to ceiling, that could be opened up to turn the room into an outdoor place in effect. The night was warm, and the windows were open now. Sleeper could see Kate Williams, dressed in riding clothes as brown as her sun-tanned skin. She was reading on a couch. The lights from the nearest lamp cast a curving brightness across her and left half of her in shadow.

Over his shoulder, Sleeper glanced this way and that. He could thank God that the girl was there, but, now that he had found her, he wanted other people on hand. She looked suddenly up as though she had felt his glance touching her. Then she sprang to her feet with a cry.

He knew the picture that he must be making, even in the dimness by the window. One sleeve was ripped away, and the brush through which Careless had dragged him had left many a rip in the old clothes. Besides, he had dried only to a general dampness that made the ragged clothes cling close to him.

"It's all right," he said. "Nothing to worry you."

"It's Sleeper," she said. "Why, Sleeper, come in . . . I mean, what do you want?"

"Nothing at all," he said. "I'd like to see your father, or the rest of the men . . ."

"Father's gone to bed. And all the hands have gone off to the *fiesta*. Why, Sleeper? What do you want?"

"They've all gone?" he echoed, feeling as though there was doom around him.

Williams himself, elderly, and cursed with a perpetual tremor of the hands — why, he would be worse than useless in the trouble that was sure to come.

There was nothing to pray for except the coming of Lowry and Lowry's men. Could he be sure that Lowry *had* men? Had that blast on the whistle meant something real?

"There's something wrong," said the girl. "Do tell me what it is. I was so sorry today, when you almost got Careless for your own horse. Sleeper, tell me what's the trouble."

"No trouble for me," he answered, stepping a short distance into the room. "But a lot of trouble ahead for you, Kate, I'm afraid."

She raised a hand suddenly to her face and peered at him. "Trouble?" she echoed. "For me?"

"Loder," he said.

The blow struck her hard. He looked vaguely over the big, barn-like room. What could he do, except strike her again.

"Do you mean . . . ?" she began.

"I know about it," he said. "I know the way you feel, too. That Charlie Loder has had a bad deal. That he's as good a man, really, as can be found."

"That *is* the truth!" she exclaimed.

"It's not the truth," said Sleeper. "I've seen him kill a man tonight . . . shoot him in the back."

He could see the words hurt her like a striking hand. Then she tossed up her head and drew in a great breath.

"Sleeper," she said, "that's a slander . . . and a lie."

"Is it?" said Sleeper, his pride not in the least hurt. "I'll name the man he killed . . . Belling."

"A thief and a man-killer! Everyone knows what Belling is!"

"Was!" he corrected. "Belling's dead, and the cataracts of the White Water have chewed him up small and fine."

"Then . . . if Charlie had a hand in it, he had to strike in self-defense," she declared.

He admired, in a strange way, this faith that she had lodged so invincibly in the outlaw. "You can see that my own clothes are a little wet," he said.

"I can see that," she answered, white-faced, frowning.

"I had to jump into the White Water to get away from Charlie Loder's gun," he said. "I had to jump . . . with my hands tied behind me."

"Sleeper! But . . . your hands tied behind you?"

"Yes."

"Above the cataract?"

He could see the direction in which her thought was moving.

"A horse saved me . . . Careless."

"A horse saved you!" she cried, utterly incredulous.

"He came for me, and I grabbed the stirrup with my teeth. Careless pulled me out. He's out there now . . . Careless . . . if you want to see him."

"Isn't it the truth that you've *stolen* Careless?" she exclaimed, "and if Charlie did anything . . . it was to a horse thief?"

Outside the house a very thin and musical whistle sounded. The girl started, turned suddenly toward the sound.

"I . . . ," she began. "I'll talk to you . . . later, Sleeper."

"You can't go to Loder," he answered.

"How do you dare to say that?" she demanded.

"He's got a fellow who looks like a minister to marry you. But it's not a real minister. He's got a real gold ring for you, and that's the only truth in what he's going to do. Will you believe me?"

"I'll never believe you!" cried the girl.

"You've got to," he answered. "I've got only seconds left, and, if Loder finds me here, he'll prove what he is . . . by murdering me, Kate."

The thin whistle sounded again, a good deal closer.

"I've got to go!" exclaimed the girl. "There can't be a word of truth in what you've said."

144

"Well, then," he said, "I'll play my last card. It probably won't be worth a thing, either." He took from inside his shirt the bit of oiled silk and drew from it the picture. Only at the edges was it wet.

"Did you know that Charlie Loder was a married man?" he asked.

She came swiftly and snatched the picture. There was no great need of question and examination. The white veil and the pretty face of the girl, the flowers in her hand, and tall Charlie Loder standing beside her — that was the story quickly enough.

"Then it's someone that he married a long time ago," she stammered. "Years and years, and she's dead . . . or they're divorced . . ."

"Does he look a lot younger in that picture?" asked Sleeper.

The girl, with a moan, slipped into the depths of a chair and lay there with her head far back, the picture trailing from one hand toward the floor. Sleeper looked away from her to find tall Charlie Loder on the farther side of the room.

The girl saw him, too. She sprang up, crying: "It isn't true, Charlie! I know it isn't true!"

Loder, disregarding her utterly, made a sufficient answer. He kept a steady, deadly eye on Sleeper and drew a revolver from beneath his coat.

CHAPTER
SEVEN

"The Trail That Never Ends"

Loder would not miss. Men said that he *could* not miss. It was three steps to reach the tall window and the dark of the night outside it. Even if only one step had been needed, it would have been too much.

Sleeper rested the finger tips of his right hand on the table beside him. There was a heavy little Mexican ashtray made of iron sitting on the table, and that would be his only weapon.

The girl said nothing, did nothing. She only stood there holding out the picture like a statue.

"Careless pulled you through, did he?" said Loder. "Well, you had all the luck that's going to be with you on one night. You're going to die, Sleeper!"

"No!" screamed the girl. "Charlie, you won't murder him!"

"Stop the yapping, you little yellow-headed fool," snarled Loder. "If I'd had the chance to get you, I would have made some dough out of that wooden-headed father of yours. But the kid smashed my game! By God, when I think of it, I don't believe it's true. I'm dreaming here, and Sleeper's where he ought to be, in

146

hell with Belling." His voice went crazy — it fell to pieces in a screech: "Take this . . . you slinking snake!"

Sleeper snatched at the iron ashtray as he ducked. He seemed to be bowing to fate, but he dipped so low that the bullet which should have smashed through his ribs and his heart only slashed his back. He side-stepped like a boxer — and ran in.

A fellow who flees merely steadies the nerves of the enemy. But no man in the world is perfectly cool against a charge. Sleeper had just about one thousandth of a second to do this thinking, and that was time enough. He hurled that heavy little iron ashtray as he dodged in. The second bullet brushed his face with hornet wings. And the ashtray clipped the side of Loder's head, as he fired the third shot. The bullet went into the wooden floor as Sleeper dived at his man.

The life of Sleeper had been rich in time; God had given him an eye faster than an antelope's heels — and now he was fighting for his life. He had a thirty pound handicap of hard muscle to overcome — plus a gun.

He got rid of the gun first — with the edge of his hand, Sleeper struck the gun hand of Loder at the wrist. The fingers of Loder opened as though on springs. The heavy Colt crashed on the floor and spun away.

That made the right hand of Loder not much good for the instant. With the left he dropped a heavy blow behind Sleeper's ear. The weight of it and the stunning impact flattened him on the floor.

He had a chance to see Loder reaching for the fallen Colt. He saw the girl, too. She had picked up a heavy poker from the fireplace, and she was running in with the long iron poised above her head in both hands. Her face was contorted out of all human semblance. She was white — a sort of stone or pale clay color. And she was screaming continually: "Murder! Murder! Murder!"

Half the brain of Sleeper was numb, but he had wit enough to use his feet where his hands could not help him. He kicked with his heel at Loder's knee and saw the big fellow slither to the floor. Sleeper, with a turn of his entire body, with a leap like that of a snake, was at his man at once.

A fist cracked him between the eyes. He got hold of that arm and gave it a sudden twist. Loder howled. They rolled over. Sleeper twisted that arm again and heard the cracking, muffled sounds of breaking bones. The scream of Loder was a frightful thing.

Then something flashed. It was the revolver that Loder had scooped up from the floor with his right hand. Sleeper swayed his head to the side. That was not enough to avoid the coming blow. He felt the thud of it. The barrel of the gun seemed to crash straight through against his brain. He could see and hear dimly, but his body was asleep.

Loder was on his feet. He knocked the iron rod out of the hands of the screaming girl, and, as it was flung away, he struck her backhanded with the barrel of the gun. She fell on her knees.

The screaming had ended. It had been like a fire, enwrapping Sleeper's half numbed brain. Now he was able to think, and he knew that he was about to die.

The left arm of Loder swayed uncertainly, crookedly. But his right hand was steady enough, holding the gun. His face was old, knotted, and twisted by an agony and by hate as though by decades of foul life.

"So this is the answer, eh?" he said.

Footfalls were hurrying down from the top part of the house.

"I'd like to take time on you," said Loder. "But I've got to hurry. By God, I'd like to take my time. I'd like to have the blonde-headed little fool awake to watch me, too."

The girl lay on her face, senseless. Sleeper had propped himself up on his hands to face the bullet.

"Right between the eyes is the surest place, Loder," he said.

Then a voice behind Loder said from one of the big open windows: "This way, Charlie!"

Loder jerked his head around over his shoulder while his gun still covered Sleeper.

There was a stocky man with unshaven red beard on his face. There was a very tall, very thin man with a foolish grin. There was a third fellow, who was Pop Lowry, the peddler. Two of them had revolvers, but old Pop carried a leveled rifle. All three guns spoke at once.

The weight of the driving lead turned Loder. He struck on his side and, turning on his back, lay dead beside Sleeper. Perhaps it was the impact of the fall that made a living sigh pass through his lips.

"And the kid?" said the unshaven man calmly.

"Leave him alone! He's saved the stuff for us!" commanded Lowry.

It was Pop Lowry who reached the fallen body of big Loder first. There was no searching to be done. Both coat pockets were bulging with the packages of money. Pop Lowry got it, turned, and fled. For the footfalls of Williams were rapidly approaching the room.

They kept Sleeper for a whole week in the Williams house, although he was ready to ride on the third day. But, since he was in a ground floor room, and since there was a bit of pasture right behind the house, he was able to lie propped up in the bed and look through the window at Careless, grazing in the sun.

Two or three times a day he would whistle, and Careless, leaping the fence, came and thrust his head in through the window. He could reach the bed of his master, and he did this with a great deal of care, snuffing loudly in protest against the smell of the iodine. Only when he had his velvet muzzle right against the hand of Sleeper would he be sure that it was, indeed, the master.

Then there was the rancher, who used to come in several times a day and spend hours chatting. He brought reports of how his daughter was convalescing during her sickness. The nerve shock had been very great, but the doctor declared that in a few weeks she would be able to travel.

"And now for you," said Williams on the seventh day. "I want to make your future my charge, Sleeper. I want you to pick out the thing you wish to do . . . and then I'll see that you have the means to do it. I don't care

150

what the scale is. What you've saved me from . . . what you've saved Kate from, to put it better . . ."

Sleeper frowned at the ceiling. "I want to thank you," he said, "but . . ."

"Don't let there be any buts," urged Williams.

"We'll remember each other kindly, and let it go at that," said Sleeper.

"My dear fellow . . . ," began Williams.

But Sleeper shook his head in such a way that the rancher understood argument would do no good.

This, perhaps, was a greater shock to Williams than anything that had ever happened in his life, including that terrible scene in his living room, when he had found a wounded man on the floor beside a dead man, and his daughter senseless, nearby.

"We want to forget this, anyway," said Sleeper. "All that people know is that Loder came to your house, to rob it, maybe. And that Sleeper happened to be going by and got drawn into the thing . . . nobody knows exactly how. And that some enemies of Loder had followed him and murdered him in the house. That's all people know. It's all that's good for them to know. If they wonder why I've got Careless . . . well, they can ask Shorty Joe Bennett to explain, if they can find Shorty . . ."

Things were left like that. When Sleeper left the Williams house on the seventh day, he rode Careless not to the town of White Water but to the little shack abandoned in the woods to the east of the town. He found the peddler with glasses on his big nose, sitting in long red underwear on a stump and sewing a patch on the seat of an old pair of trousers.

Pop Lowry looked up from threading a needle and then pushed his glasses high up on his forehead. "Well, well, well!" he said. "I been waiting for you all of these days. And here you are!"

"Here I am for pay day," said Sleeper.

"Pay day?" exclaimed the peddler in great surprise. "You got Careless, didn't you? Ain't he worth more than the thousand dollars I was gonna give you?"

Sleeper smiled kindly down at Pop Lowry. "Look here, Pop," he said, "I did a few things more than you asked me to do."

"That's me," said Lowry. "I always throw in enough to make folks satisfied, over and above what they pay for."

"I've given you more than a thousand dollars' worth of silence," said Sleeper. "Suppose that I let people know that Pop Lowry has just collected at least half of a hundred and ten thousand dollars? Suppose I let them know that he had hold of Belling . . . and let him get away? Suppose I let them know that Pop Lowry only has to blow a whistle and a crowd of gunmen come out of the woods? Wouldn't they wonder why Pop keeps on wandering around through the mountains with his three mules?"

Pop Lowry sighed. "How come that you never done any talking, Sleeper?" he asked. He drew a purse from his pocket and took almost all the bills that were in it. These he passed to Sleeper. "I would have thought," said Lowry, "that you'd've wanted to make a hero out

152

of yourself, Sleeper. You've done enough to sit high the rest of your life, if you only talked a little."

"People that sit up high can't whittle a stick and enjoy the sunshine," said Sleeper.

The peddler laughed. "You're a queer one, Sleeper," he said. "You gonna go right on, the same old way?"

"Are you going to keep packing your mules and selling stuff cheap . . . because you've got no overhead, Pop?" countered Sleeper.

The peddler scratched his chin and finally permitted himself a very broad smile. Sleeper was smiling, also.

TIMBER LINE

"Timber Line" was originally published in Street & Smith's *Western Story Magazine* under the Max Brand byline in the issue dated November 24, 1923. The story opens with the hero, known only as Jerney, riding into a fierce winter storm in the mountains. Jerney's predicament only worsens as the tale of mistaken identity and revenge unfolds in a cabin in which he takes refuge. Among the cabin's pathetically poor family members is the heroine, Marie Rochambeau, a glimmer of light for both Jerney and the reader. This marks the first appearance of "Timber Line" since its original publication.

CHAPTER ONE

"Madame Leads The Way"

The wind struck Jerney when he climbed out of the foothills, and, when he looked above him, he saw that the mountaintops were black with the storm. If he had been an old mountaineer, he would have stopped at that point and slept at the village. In fact, tenderfoot though he was, he could not help noting that, when he mounted again at the village and started off toward the highlands, more than one of the men and women he passed looked at him and then to the upper levels with a frown of concern.

He did not, however, turn back, but held steadily on, for he was a man who clung to a purpose, even a small one, with a bulldog tenacity. He had planned to cross the first range on this day, and it was impossible for him to give up his scheme and his schedule. Moreover, he was a different man from the pale fellow who had begun this horseback tour. His cheeks were thin, but no longer pale. The sun had embrowned his hands to such a degree that, when he looked down to them on the reins, he wondered at them; they were the hands of a stranger. The fatigue of the saddle, which had been a deadly thing at first, no longer troubled him, and he

157

could pass ten hours on the back of a horse without trouble.

This happened in the first fortnight. In the next ten days he began to gain so much in strength that he sat erect in the saddle by choice and involuntarily, as it were, although he had slumped into a shapeless figure at first. His flabby muscles had turned hard. The crease of worry and nerves between his eyes disappeared. The eyes themselves grew clear and sharp. Only his forehead was still pale, but the lower part of his face was almost as brown as the backs of his hands. The back of his neck was no longer burned raw; it had become leathery.

In the meantime, Madame had taught him how to ride. He had called the mustang by that name because an imperious way she had of tossing her head reminded him of a certain lady of his acquaintance. She resembled that haughty dame in other particulars, for she was a beautiful creature with mustang written only in her eye, just as the real madame was lovely beyond words, but with a certain look that now and again struck men dumb and caused a little chill of apprehension to pass up their spines. And it was the devil in the eyes of the mare that had made Jerney pick her out from the herd in the corral. The good-natured dealer warned him frankly against her, but Jerney persisted. He spent a bitter first week there at the ranch, learning to stick in the saddle. In that time, he estimated that she had pitched him out of his stirrups four times a day, and, although the ground was cushioned inches deep in velvety dust, he was a mass of bruises and sprains before he had done. But, on the seventh day, he managed to stay in the saddle, and on the eighth he began his long journey.

There were troubles with Madame, thick and long continued. For the first fortnight she tossed him over her head or slid him off her rump on an average of twice a day, but, after he was fallen, she never wandered far away. Sometimes it required two or three hours of patient work before she could be caught, but she always submitted at last, as though she balanced the pleasure of freedom against the pleasure of tormenting this foolish master, and at length the latter outbalanced the former joy.

After three weeks of constant effort, Jerney came to know her more exactly than he had ever known the mind of a man or a woman or a child; he could tell by the way she regarded him in the morning what her attitude would be during the day. He knew by a certain tremor in her ears when she was preparing to rid herself of the burden of his weight. And when her legs turned into limber springs beneath him, he knew that a grim burst of bucking was to follow. He even began to be able to guess the very form her bucking would take. Sometimes he knew with utter certainty that he had nothing but fencrowing to contend with. Sometimes, in a most devilish humor, she would vary straight bucking by rearing and hurling herself backward to grind him between the pommel and the hard ground. And sometimes she varied her efforts by some sunfishing of the most bone-breaking variety.

In the end, the great day came when she performed for a whole half hour, and at the end of that time Jerney was dizzy, sick, with an aching brain and eyes starting from his head. But Madame was thoroughly and whole-heartedly beaten. When she stopped her performance and dropped her head and tail, he slashed her cruelly with the quirt. Behold! Instead of diving at the sun above them, she merely broke into a weak-legged canter. He slashed her again. The canter only became a little faster, and she snorted a faint protest to the third cut of the whip.

Madame was conquered at last! The heart of Jerney swelled with an immense joy. The winning of no friend had meant so much to him. The completion of no successful business stroke so exalted him. But he did not let the victory end there. Having at last met force with force, having been instructed by Madame, as it were, in the very methods which were most necessary to defeat herself, he straightway set about winning her heart, just as he had subdued her spirit. For the danger from Madame, after her surrender, was the danger of guerrilla warfare. She was a treacherous creature, full of stratagems and wiles, ready to leap sidewise, apparently in fear of a time-whitened stump, but really to unseat him; she was ready to try for his head with her heels, when he was out of the saddle; and she would snap with her teeth like a wolf. To conquer her by force and skill had been hard; to win her heart was even harder. But Jerney threw himself whole-heartedly into the struggle. In fact, when he should have been enjoying the mountains, he was studying Madame, and he studied her with such success that, at length, he was able to make her his friend. And on one happy morning

160

he saw her lift her head, when she sighted him, and heard her whinny a welcome.

What was the other triumph compared with this? Thereafter, their rides were most conversational. She would keep a ear canted back as though to listen to his words, and, talking softly to Madame, he wound along the trails with never a lonely moment. There were no treacherous side-steps now, no bucking in the morning when he mounted, but all went smoothly as a song for Jerney. And if the nervous mare cocked her ears at a difficult bit of trail and began to tremble, he could soothe her like a child with the gentle touch of his voice. He had come to have the most absolute trust in her, for she was born and bred to the mountains. Her hard, round hoofs were as sure as the feet of a mule, and she had a mule's uncanny endurance and wisdom, united with all the spirit of a horse and a swinging gallop worthy of a Thoroughbred.

So it was that Jerney looked up to the storm-wrapped tops of the mountains on this day and made no doubt but that he could cross them and gain the shelter of the valley beyond, before night.

He miscalculated twice, however. In the first place, he trusted the estimate of distances that the villagers gave him; in the second place, he misjudged the angle of the mountainsides before him, They stretched long arms easily toward the foothills. They seemed simple enough for climbing until he was actually beneath them, and then they arose like a wall above him and blotted away half of the heavens. Still he went on, putting implicit trust in Madame, and she went

161

gallantly at her work. As always, when he was in a tight place, he gave her the rein, and she followed her own head; in five minutes she had located an obscure trail and was working her way up it. The higher they climbed, the more often the wind struck them.

At mid-afternoon the darkness lifted from the peaks. Jerney saw the cloud masses torn apart as the wind changed to a new direction; the masses of mist tumbled down to the shoulders of the sky, and there banked along the horizon. The sun shone dazzlingly bright, and the bald rock heads of the range flashed with water and sun like polished metal.

Even if the journey should last into the night, thought Jerney, the bright starlight would make it very possible to go on with such a sure-footed, wise-headed horse as Madame to carry him. But he changed his mind to a degree, when he reached the upper levels. He found himself in a strange and monstrous scene of beauty. For the wind had been steadily gathering in strength during the last hour or so, and now it was a gale of such terrible violence that he could not present his face to it. He had to dismount and stride ahead with his head canted to the side and his broad-brimmed hat pulled down low. Even so the terrific and cutting power of that storm flapped the brim of the hat against his face so keenly that it was like the lashings of a whip.

It was not a steady torrent of air, for the level stream of wind above was sluiced away down the cañons of the mountains, reflected from wall to wall of the ravines, and so cannoned out against Jerney from changing directions. Now it smote him in the face and stopped

162

him in his tracks, and again it staggered him from the side with a blow like a club. Sometimes it cut in behind him, lifted him to his tiptoes, and gave wings to his steps. His body became a thing of feathers at such time.

Madame, in the meantime, followed him like a dog. She was highly disturbed, and sometimes she came up to nudge at his shoulder with her muzzle and beg a reassuring word that could not be heard, even though he shouted, against the awful cannonading of that storm. Every foot of headway he made was at the cost of a tremendous expenditure of strength. But he had strength and to spare, now; he began to reap the fruit of the temperate, physically busy, and mentally placid life of the past weeks. His legs began to ache, but they did not tremble; his eyes blurred, but they did not grow weak. And there were such things to use those eyes upon as he had never dreamed were born between heaven and earth.

The storm he had witnessed blackening the top of the range had been a thick downpour of snow that piled high on the top of other masses of snow, all dried and sifted and turned to thinnest powder by the wind that had been blowing like a breath from the Arctic for the past few days. But that wind had not yet been strong enough to disturb the great, fluffy masses and drifts of snow which choked the crevasses and chasms with white feathers, hundreds of feet deep, and flooded every wide hollow. This wind giant, however, was now rousing that snow from the deepest bottoms. It poured it forth in vast and level-driven quantities that traveled ahead at an undreamed of pace until the current of snow-laden wind reached the slope of a mountain. Up that slope it raced, reached the top of the peak, and then flooded out into the empty space beyond like smoke pouring from so many funnels.

Jerney saw a hundred monstrous mountain heads around him, and from the top of every one there floated an enormous snow banner, thick and rounded at its base where it was attached to the summit, and then spreading wider and flatter and thinner until it had reached out for a mile, perhaps, growing incandescent toward the broad fringe, taking the sunlight in changing and transparent colors, and finally streaming out to nothing. From the edges of that waving flag masses of the snow dust snapped off, from time to time, and streaked away across the heavens. But while the wind harried the sky, the sun still shone brighter and brighter as it sank toward the west, and went down, finally, and cast across the hundred banners a glow of rose and gold. It was a sight to see and die for.

But now all changed as suddenly as it had come into being. In a trice the wind fell away. The snow flags flapped heavily, and then dropped to the ground. And, blowing gently from a new quarter, the wind picked up the serried hosts of the clouds which had lingered gloomily upon the horizon all this time and rolled them rapidly back across the sky. In half an hour the twilight was dimmed and smudged to the dark of night. When night itself came, the mountains would be as black as the heart of a cavern. Jerney looked gloomily about him, recognized that he had brought himself and his horse into a great peril, and considered what was to be done.

For the cold had not abated. It had not the poniard point that the storm had given it, but, still, it was intense enough to be dangerous, if they stopped moving for a moment. It would make the circulation sluggish, and soon it would bring on that hideous drowsiness that is the precursor of death by freezing. Yet, they could not continue to trek on all through the night. He was very tired. The good mare was even more worn. And now the anxieties of picking a way through the night among chasms and crevasses was added to the dangers of cold and exhaustion.

Already the trail was become so dim that to Jerney it was merely a nightmare path, winding through the darkness of a dream. So he gave gallant Madame her head once more and let her what she would.

First of all she stood still, and, as the chill of the wind began to work into his blood, he thought for one dreadful moment that her spirit was gone, and that she had surrendered to the inevitable. But her attitude was not that of despondency. She bore her head high, and, apparently, she was merely taking her bearings in that mysterious and inexplicable manner which some animals have. Then she turned sharply to the left and went straight into the teeth of the storm.

Jerney, amazed and alarmed, reached for the reins, but she shook her head at this, as though she would caution him to keep his head out of this business and not trouble her with suggestions. Indeed, she went on as steadily as though she were following a light invisible to him. She went on to the very edge of a precipice and then wandered along it among rough rocks, while Jerney had not the courage to look into the well of watery blackness that told of the gorge beside them. And it was darker now than he had dreamed it possible to become. They were traveling through a mist of low-blowing clouds, turning to soft snow as it touched the vicinity of the rocks. He could barely see the withers of Madame. Her head was quite lost to him.

Leaning back in the saddle helplessly, he let her take him on, with a hideous certainty that, sooner or later, her foot would slip, and they would both lurch into the gully beside them.

But there was no slip. Presently she turned out of the face of the wind, and, making another angle with her former course, she left the force of the storm on the farther side of the mountain, and Jerney heard it howling and shouting far above his head and in the distance, as though rumbling in the bowels of the mountain and trying to come through at him. Immediately about him there was only the thick mist, and this was lightening a little. Now and again he could see the head of Madame. And when he spoke, he could see her ears prick as ever to answer him.

His heart went out to her in gratitude and in wonder, also, as it might have gone out to another man, stronger and wiser than he, who was guiding him through a veritable abyss of danger. He blessed the lucky star that had led him to her in the midst of the other horses in the corral.

166

When I see Madame again, he thought to himself, *I shall tell her that she has saved my life. She will think that I have gone mad to accuse her of having ever saved anything.*

They were now following a definite trail that apparently was the thing which Madame had guessed at when she was so far away among the mountains. It descended steadily, winding along the side of the mountain. Although it was narrow enough and doubled back and forth among the rocks like a hunted fox, yet it was a safe and easy course compared with some of the going which they had seen on this day. The nerves of Jerney grew quieter and quieter. His trust in the wisdom of Madame was now the trust which he would have put in a man, or it was, even more, as though he recognized in her instincts beyond the wisdom of the mortal mind.

Then, in the midst of the descent, with the air growing warmer every moment and the mist less thick, she stopped abruptly. He craned his neck and could make out the trail extending straight before them. What could be wrong? He urged her with his voice. She would not stir. He slapped her with his voice. She would not stir. He slapped her flank; she only shook her head.

"A foolish whim," said Jerney aloud. "I'll have to take her in hand." And he prepared at once for sterner measures.

CHAPTER
TWO

"The Trap"

He took Madame on a short rein, gathered the quirt in his fingers, and tapped her lightly with it. She crouched and trembled as though she felt the wound far more in spirit than in body. But she did not stir an inch ahead. Then, a little angered at this return of her old stubbornness, he cut her smartly with the quirt.

Madame, with a snort of fear and pain, reared and leaped high into the air, flinging herself forward as far as she could. Her forefeet landed solidly and safely. But when the rear hoofs struck, the ground gave sickeningly beneath them, and Jerney felt the staunch body beneath him sink.

He was out of the saddle in the winking of an eye and fell prone on the ground beside her. She hung by half her body and her forelegs upon a ledge. Her hindquarters dangled into nothingness, and a twelve-foot section of the trail behind her had fallen away. Only now, minutes, it seemed, after her leap, there rose from far beneath them the rumbling sound of a mass of earth and rubble landing heavily. Had it not been for the gallant effort of Madame, he and she would have been a part of that fall.

168

Jerney would have fainted with that horror had there not been so urgent a need for action. The good mare was struggling, but making no progress toward drawing herself up to safety. So he jumped to her head, caught the reins, and threw all his weight and his lifting power into an effort that made his back crack. And with that powerful lift to help her, Madame edged the forward part of her body a little more onto the shelf of rock which had received her, scrambled like a cat, and so raised herself, at last, to the firm footing. There she stood, cowering against the rock wall of the mountain, quite unnerved. When Jerney stepped back, she followed him hastily and thrust her head against him like a child asking for comfort.

It was many minutes before they proceeded. He lighted matches and made out that she had been scratched along the belly by the rocks, but not deeply cut. Then, with voice and hand, he quieted her until her trembling had ceased. Finally he went down the trail again with Madame following behind him so closely that her forehoofs tapped at his heels, and now and again she would lift and turn her head, as though the danger had come to life and was apt to follow them.

But the trail now broadened, and presently it sloped off into a narrow valley in which they could hear the rushing and calling of a watercourse multiplied by echoes. They came to the level, and he mounted again, while Madame went forward with a renewed courage. Luck was with them at the last, however, for as they wound among a dense growth of trees, a light winked before them, and they came out into a clearing before a long, low-built house. No palace could have appeared so pleasant to the eye of Jerney; the weariness which he had fought out of his brain now overtook him in a wave and made him weak in an instant.

When he tapped at the door, it was opened at once, and a great loutish fellow of eighteen years or so looked out at him with a frightened face, one hand holding the bolt of the door and the other grasping a rifle.

"What's here?" he asked, half frightened and half angry.

"I've lost my way," said Jerney. "I've lost my way coming over the mountains and into the storm. Can you put me up for the night?"

"We got no room," said the fellow, and therewith slammed the door in his face.

Jerney was too amazed to act at once. He had traveled far through the West by this time and had put up at many a place among men of rough words and rough ways, but he had never yet encountered either unkindness or inhospitableness. And now there was a click of iron inside the door as this odd mountaineer began to bolt his door as against an intruder.

Jerney acted without forethought. He put his weight behind the padding muscle of his left shoulder and struck the door. There was a gritting of iron, and the door flew wide. It struck the breast of the fellow within and catapulted him back so that he staggered halfway across the room and then tripped and sat down hard, while the rifle fell with a clatter from his hand.

He was not alone in the room. It was a long, low apartment which obviously served at once as a dining room and kitchen. Over the rusted and staggering stove in the farther end a bedraggled woman was leaning, and a boy of fourteen sat like a brown-faced young Indian, cross-legged in the warmest corner, half asleep. A white-faced girl in her early twenties had started up at this intrusion. A huge dog, half mastiff and half wolfhound, had risen with a lion-like roar to fly at the intruder.

Jerney picked up the fallen rifle. "Call off your dog," he commanded, "or I'll kill the brute. Do you hear me? Call him off!"

"Sam!" called the hag who now turned from the stove. "Call Tom off!"

For big Tom was coming straight at the stranger, growling like a demon, with his lips twitched back from a mouthful of fangs.

"Steady, Tom," said the boy called Sam, scrambling to his feet. "Stay, boy! Damn you!" he added fiercely, as the dog kept straight on in spite of the call.

At this last command the big dog hesitated, stopped, and then slunk across the room and took shelter behind his young master, still rumbling a threat deep in his throat and peering out as if he yearned to be at the intruder.

"This is an odd performance," said Jerney, looking sternly about him. "If you haven't room for me, direct me to the nearest house or town. But to close your door in the face of a traveler on a night like this . . ." He paused and waited.

"There's no telling who's out on a night like this," said the woman of the house by way of apology. "It

171

ain't always friends that comes and raps on the doors of honest folks. We got to take care of ourselves. We got to do that, don't we?"

"Of course," admitted Jerney. "Of course, you do."

He closed out some of the wind and the rain by partially shutting the door behind him, for the rain was now streaking down in torrents, as though a million hoses were playing from the skies.

"Only," he said, "give me directions for going on down the valley."

"Follow the stream," said the elder boy, while the younger now recovered his wits from sleep and rose to his feet. "Follow along the stream. Ain't anything can take you wrong. You'll come to a house about two mile farther down."

"Why," said the girl, breaking in suddenly, "you know that there ain't a house inside fifteen mile, Sam!"

Sam favored the girl with an ugly look, and the hag at the stove called with a snarl: "Shut your face and mind your tongue, Marie. There ain't been no call for you to talk."

Yet, fifteen miles or five, any amount of travel would have been more welcome to Jerney than a night spent in the bosom of this wolfish family, but his eye caught on Marie, and held there. For women had ever been the weakness of Jerney; a pretty face was to him a lodestone of irresistible power to attract him, and now he saw a rare beauty, indeed. She was dressed in rags no better than those which clad the others in the room, but they were clean rags, at least, and cleanliness in such surroundings was more than a virtue — it was a miracle. The sun which had blackened the faces of the boys had merely darkened hers to a rich olive, into which the recent excitement had brought up a rich flush and set a light in her black eyes. She was slim and supple of make. He could tell by a glance that she was as light-faced as any boy, and well-nigh as strong. Now she bore the reproof of the woman with a shrug of indifference. But she did not speak again.

There was no need for more words, however. Jerney, after that first look at her, had made up his mind that, if the house were filled with wolves in very truth, he would nevertheless spend the night among them for the sake of seeing more of this wild beauty.

"Fifteen miles?" he said. "It's a long cry for a tired man. Fifteen miles through this wild night with a tired horse? It can't be done. Good people, I'll pay you well. And I ask nothing but a shelter for my horse and a spot on the floor where I may lie down. These things I must have. I see some sheds outside . . . there must be a corner in one of them where Madame can be stalled. And you, Sam, will be glad to show it to me, I know."

Sam and the woman exchanged significant glances, and then she shrugged her shoulders, a movement which sickened Jerney as he thought how like had been the shrug of the girl. Was she, indeed, an offspring of this family of beasts?

"Come along," said Sam. "I'll show you."

He went out into the night with Jerney.

CHAPTER
THREE

"Sheltered"

Sam carried a lantern and led the way to a low, long shed in the rear of the house. When he opened the door, the sweet smell of hay was thick about them, and Madame sniffed the air with hungry nostrils. There were three other horses already stabled here, ragged-maned, stunted creatures, gaunt with ill usage and hard work. They laid their ears back at the sight of men, but Jerney was presently too busy, taking care of Madame, to pay any heed to them.

First he brought her half a bucket of water — she was too hot for the moment to have more. Then he filled her manger with hay, and into the feed box in the corner of the manger he poured a small measure of barley. Then, with wisps of the hay, he rubbed her down, having unsaddled her, and swished away sweat and rain water together, working with such patient care that Sam shifted half a dozen times from one foot to the other and yawned as he held his lantern.

"Look here, mister," he said at length, "d'you do this every night?"

"Why," said Jerney, "don't you, when you've ridden your horse all day?"

"The devil, no," said Sam. "Hosses are cheap, I reckon, and a man's time ain't. That's what Pa says. He remembers times when you could pick up a good hoss for five dollars. Hosses are cheaper'n cows."

"It isn't the price," explained Jerney. "It's the honest work they do for you. If she's brought me safely through, I can only make her comfortable."

"She looks comfortable, right enough," admitted Sam, looking Madame over carefully. "She's a pretty thing, ain't she?"

"I'd call her a beauty."

"Fast?"

"As the wind!"

"Don't look like she'd last, though."

"Does she seem spent to you now?"

"Not what I'd call tired out. When I'm through with a beast, it looks like it'd been plumb beat . . ."

"Yet she carried me from Alder Town today."

"Today?"

"Yes."

"Well," said Sam, "you don't mean that you rode her across the range?"

"Yes."

"She's got wings, then," said Sam stubbornly. "Otherwise, it ain't in hossflesh to do it." A new idea came to him. "You crossed the range, eh?"

"Yes."

"Why, dog-gone it, the only way off the range into the valley is along the trail . . ."

"Comes into the bottom a mile from your house . . . that's the way we traveled."

"You . . . ," Sam choked and stopped.

"Why?" asked Jerney.

"Oh, nothin'. You come down the trail, eh?" he added more to himself than to Jerney, and, when the latter again asked him why he was so curious and surprised, the boy broke out: "Anything happen on the trail? Anything queer, I mean?"

It startled Jerney. "Part of it had been underwashed by the rains, I guess," he said. "A section of it gave way under us."

"Ah," murmured Sam. "And . . . how in the name of mighty did you keep from going down, too?"

It was all so recent and fresh in the mind of Jerney that it half sickened him even to speak or think of it, but now he described it all — how Madame had halted, how the whip had made her jump, and how the ground had given way behind her and she herself had barely reached safety on the farther side. Sam listened with a breathless interest, his little black eyes glittering out at the stranger beneath his long and brushy forelock.

"I understand now," he said, "why you're so dog-gone particular with her. If had a hoss that could read the mind of a mountain trail, maybe I'd be special kind to 'em, too."

They started back for the house. The sleepiness had quite deserted Sam now. He was on fire with interest. He could not learn enough about the mare and how she had been trained. Such a horse, he said, was worth her weight in gold — or more than that. In return for the information he gave, Jerney asked him about the family. It was his mother who was cooking, Sam told

176

him. His brother Harry was the boy by the stove, and the girl was Marie Rochambeau, from Canada. She had come to them as an infant, when her father and mother died, because these were her only relatives, no matter how distant. They had been kind to her.

They reached the house as Jerney learned this, and it seemed to him that his very heart was lightened by the tidings. It was the lifting of a black imputation of stain and bad blood from the reputation of the girl. And yet, he told himself, he had guessed before that she could not belong by blood to this tribe of wild men.

In the long room he found Marie alone and working busily at the stove. Harry had gone to bed; Mrs. Larson was preparing sleeping quarters for their guest. It was the duty of Marie to prepare his supper. A venison steak now smoked in the frying pan; the coffee pot was beginning to steam; and a sodden chunk of home-made whole wheat bread lay on the table beside a tin plate and a tin cup. There was no cloth upon the table, but that place had been newly scrubbed and dried; it made a white spot on the surface, compared with the grimy rest of the table. Jerney knew that it had been cleaned in his honor, and he looked with a new interest at Marie Rochambeau.

The heat of the stove had flushed her, and her thick, lustrous hair, which was chopped off short at the nape of the neck, flew abroad as she turned hastily here and there in her work, reaching for the salt and pepper, or jerking the door of the firebox open to throw in new wood, or standing back to wave the smoke of the cookery away from her eyes.

To Jerney the fragrance of the cooking meat was a most delicious perfume, and the girl by the stove was half wild Indian, half classic nymph. He looked about him. The lout, Sam, had left the room again, carrying his rifle under his arm. And Jerney was alone with Marie Rochambeau.

He began to feel the conversational quality which exists in the very air, as it were, when two people are alone together. The entrance of a third destroys the magic. People begin to talk, not to feel and think. For to talk with two is to talk for an audience; one acts a part behind footlights. To talk with one is to talk with oneself. Conversation cannot be avoided; the very silence is eloquent. It is in vain that two solitary men in a railroad coach strive to be oblivious of one another. The presence of each presses in upon the other. But in a crowd every man is alone.

So it was that Jerney, when he was alone with the girl, felt his heartbeat quickening. Yet he did not look at her at first, but around the room at other objects. And everything was talking, not of itself alone, but of Marie Rochambeau, also. It was a true frontiersman's home, when the frontier is stripped to its naked truth and not expressed in pleasant fictions. Old clothes hung from nails along the walls, that were unpainted and, of course, unpapered. The wind, prying through various notches, put those clothes into faint motion. The faded blue jumper put out its arms as though a ghost had stepped into it. And the leather coat, rubbed full of holes, swayed back and forth with a light whispering. There were guns, too, but mostly rusted and beyond use. For the negligence of the mountaineers took care of the newest weapons only, and let the others fall quickly into disrepair. There were old traps of sundry sizes, looking like rusty fetters. And there were half a dozen pictures cut out of papers and pasted up. They were faded and stained with rain which had trickled through the roof and worked its way down the sides of the walls. Although they were now unrecognizable, the inhabitants of the house had been too lazy and careless to scrape them off again.

Yet, in this setting, the girl had grown up tall and beautiful and strong and with a certain freshness about her that seemed to distinguish her from all the others of womankind. It was a dark background which made her loveliness more rare. Now he turned directly upon her at the very moment that she, in lifting the venison steak from the pan to his tin plate, raised her eyes to meet his. And, at once, her glance sank. She approached the table shamefacedly and put down the plate without being able to look at him again. Jerney felt his own color rise. That knowledge made him at once feel foolish and angry with himself. He could not even find his voice to thank her, and so he drew up the stool — blackened by much handling — and sat down to his dinner.

The venison was wonderfully tender, cooked with a stiff crust by the great heat of the pan, and then allowed to finish more slowly, so that all the rich juices were retained within. Yet it was tasteless food to Jerney. He was cudgeling his wretched brain and striving to find something to say to the girl. She now sat on a bundle of bedding on the farther side of the room, sewing at a pair of trousers and putting a great patch across a tattered hole in the knee. Yet he knew that, when his eyes were lowered to his plate, she was looking up and aside at him, studying him.

The silence became more and more a weight. He choked down the last morsels, drained his coffee cup, and faced her rather desperately.

"I've been thinking of a lot of things I want to say to you," he confessed, "but they run into a heap, and I can't pick out the right ones."

She laid down her sewing, folded her hands on her lap, and smiled frankly at him. "I'm mighty glad you want to talk," she said. "Most of our time here is salted away with silence, d'you see?"

She had stuff in her, he decided, and the right sort of stuff. If her language was the language of men and her accent drawling, nevertheless, her mind was right. There was neither sullenness nor stupidity nor frozen self-consciousness.

"I was wondering what you did with your time," he asked her, "with no one within fifteen miles of your house?"

At this she frowned, as though surprised by the question. "Why," she said, "I'll tell a man that I don't rust for want of being used. I do what everybody around here does . . . hunt, trap, fish, chop trees for firewood . . . that sort of thing. I do what the men do, and, when they're through and sit down, I got to lend a hand with the housework. I guess that about fills in the day. Eh?" And she laughed with perfect good nature.

180

Was she contented with her lot, then? He looked sharply at her, but, when the laughter ended, there remained a little crease between her eyes, and her jaw was set hard. No, it was plain that she understood that there were other things worth having in this world.

"You do all those things?"

"That's only half."

He glanced at her hands. They were very slenderly made, but something in her gesture made him guess that they were strong as the hands of a man. They were used to gripping things and holding hard.

"You even swing an axe?" he asked, breaking into the silence that had begun to form again.

"Not like Uncle Tom," she replied at once. "I can't sink it right into a tree up to the haft, the way he can. But I'll lay ten to one that I can do more tricks than he ever dreamed of."

With that she glanced about her, and then scooped up an axe that rested against the wall nearby. She caught it three-quarters of the way up the handle and flung it suddenly from her, not with the restricted and cramped motion of an ordinary woman, but as freely overhand as any man. Before the startled eyes of Jerney, the axe shot across the room in swift circles and then struck the heavy post beside the door with a jar that shook the room and attested the power with which the heavy tool had been thrown. It did not fall with a clatter. The very bit of the steel had struck the face of the wood and sunk deep.

"Hey!" yelled the voice of the woman of the house from above. "What's that damn' foolishness down there?"

"Go on!" replied the girl in savage reply. "What's bothering you?"

She crossed the room with that supple step he had noted before. It was like the stride of a young Indian, light and strong. The axe, deeply sunken though it was, she wrested from the wood with the knack of a slight twist that worked it free.

"Sure," said Marie Rochambeau, "I can handle an axe. I was raised hefting one, I guess." And she swung the one she carried very much as a young dandy might have spun his cane. She tossed the axe back into place and sat down again as unconcernedly as though what she had done was not worth comment or afterthought.

"You ain't prospecting?" she asked him.

"No."

"Just passing through?"

"Yes."

"Where from, stranger?"

"New York was the beginning of my trip."

"New York?" She canted back her head, and while the dull lantern light flowed and gleamed along her round throat, her eyes dreamed far away to that great and strange city. "Well," she sighed at last, "that's a mighty long trek, I'd tell a man. Where you bound?"

"Just passing through."

"Passing through," murmured the girl, and fell into a melancholy fit of thought so profound that, when he spoke to her again, she did not hear him.

At this moment the woman of the house climbed down from the ladder that communicated with the attic story of the building and told him that a bed was ready for him when he pleased to retire.

CHAPTER
FOUR

"Mistaken For 'Timber Line'"

He had rather have given up a year of life, at that moment, than an opportunity to prolong the conversation for another five minutes, but there was now nothing for him to do but to climb the ladder and let the woman show him to his bunk that had been rolled down at one end of a long, low room, the air of which was close and ill-smelling. There were several other bunks over which he stumbled on the way to the one that the woman pointed out to him — from one the voice of Harry cursed, shrill and sharp, at him.

He found it at last.

Jerney lay down, feeling that he was sleeping in a den of thieves in very deed. But, when he had pulled off his riding boots and thrown the blanket loosely around him, he had hardly time to make a note of the hardness of the boards upon which he was lying, for sleep-rushed out of the corners of his weary brain and presently drowned him in darkness. The last thing he heard was the moan and whistle of the rising wind that had shifted again since his arrival and was not hurling straight down the valley. He heard that. The lantern of the woman, as she retreated down the ladder, cast a dull light across the ceiling and revealed the smoky rafters and showed an immense spider's web extended across the ceiling just above his head. Then the lantern disappeared. In that moment Jerney was soundly asleep and dreaming that he and Madame were still crossing the crest of the range and leaning into the icy arms of the wind.

As for the woman, she was younger in body than in dirty, wrinkled face. She went down the ladder with the agility of a sailor, and, when she was in the living room of the hovel, she went straight to the girl.

"Look here," she said, "what was you and him talking about, so busy and thick?"

"Heaven," said the girl. She sat with her chin resting upon one brown, doubled fist, and she did not lift her sullen eyes from the floor as the other addressed her.

"Heaven?" said the crone. "What d'you mean by that? Heaven, you fool?"

"What I mean you'd never understand. Let it go at that."

"Mind how you talk to me. Mind how you talk to your aunt, Marie."

"Aunt, the devil," said Marie. "There ain't enough of your blood running into me to choke a grasshopper with. Get out of my way. You're cutting away the warmth of the stove."

The hag stepped back from her with a gleam in her eyes. "You ugly-minded brat!" she said snarlingly. "I'll learn you to give me lip. When your uncle comes home, I'll tell him the kind of talk you give me . . . by the heavens, I ain't going to wait till he comes."

And, rushing in a fury upon the girl, she laid her hands upon the shoulders of Marie. The latter, however, did not move except to lift her head and eye the other with a sort of disgusted calmness.

"Take off your hands," she said. "You're dirty. Your hands are dirty . . . and so are you. Soap an' water ain't going to take it out. It's rubbed into the grain of you. It's in your heart!"

The woman of the house reeled back, fairly choked and gasping with her fury.

"I'll wait for Tom!" she gasped out. "It's a pile better that I should wait for him. He'll handle you . . . oh, he'll handle you, when he hears how you been repayin' me for all the pain and the trouble that I've spent over you all these years. All the backaches and the heartaches that you've given me . . . and now . . ."

"Shut up," said the girl dryly. "I've heard that lingo all before, but it don't wash out and leave no color in the pan. Trouble over me? I know how you raised me. The only time you looked at me was to kick me out of your way. The only talking you did was to rave at Uncle Tom and bark at him, because he'd sent for me to take me in. You think I was too young . . . or maybe you thought I'd disremember them things? Nope, I wrote 'em all down on the insides of me, and they won't never rub out."

The hag was, for the moment, silenced. Physical violence, for which the twitching of her long fingers showed that she longed, was momentarily out of her power. She knew, apparently, without asking for a demonstration, all of the power that lay in the slender, rounded body of the girl.

She said presently: "It's this gent that's put these here ideas into your head, I reckon."

The girl shrugged her shoulders and returned to her contemplation of the knothole in the floor that had occupied her before.

"He looks sort of fine to you, maybe?"

"He looks . . . clean," said the girl at last, as though she were willing to talk on this consuming topic, even with her aunt.

"Hmm," brooded the crone. "You've lost your head, that's plain. Don't be a fool, Marie. Don't go busting your heart about him. Why, you little numbskull, don't you know who he is?"

"Ah?" said the girl, strangely moved at this. "Do *you* know anything about him?"

The other studied the lighted face beneath her with a mixture of scorn and hatred and pity that was strange to see.

"Sure I know him. I guess you'll listen to me now?"

"Tell me!"

"Plumb full of anxiousness now, ain't you?"

"Talk or not," said Marie. "I ain't going to worry. I've never heard you say anything yet that was worth listening to. I ain't going to expect nothing now."

A snarl was the answer, but the opportunity of inflicting pain was too much for the woman to resist.

"I can put what you want to know in two words," she said.

"Lemme hear 'em, then?"

"Timber Line!"

The words had a great effect, indeed. It made Marie Rochambeau stiffen and grow pale, but she recovered her breath in another moment and shook her head violently.

"What's he got to do with Timber Line?"

"Enough," said the elder woman. "He's him!"

"Timber Line? You're crazy!"

"Hear me talk, Marie. I say it's Timber Line. He's due. And he's got Timber Line's looks."

"Not inside a mile of 'em. Timber Line is a big man."

"What about this gent? He's an inch over six feet. His head brushed the rafters upstairs. I stood and watched mighty careful."

"Sure, he's tall, but that don't mean nothing. There's no broadness to him."

"What about it?"

"Everything. Timber Line's as strong as a tiger."

"Maybe this gent is, too. It ain't always the big ones that are the strong ones. There's Bill Riley. I seen him lift seven hundredweight of old iron junk and put it on a scales. And Riley ain't nothing but flesh and bones."

The girl frowned, but she was only in doubt for a moment. "This here feller come from New York."

"How d'you know?"

"He said so."

"You're a fool, Marie. You believe what he said?"

"Besides, he talked like it."

"That's Timber Line, I tell you. Talked smooth. Just like a book, Tom says."

188

"D'you think that Timber Line would dare to come in here . . . to Uncle Tom's house?"

"Why not? He knowed that Uncle Tom was away."

"He'd never dare!"

"Dare? There ain't nothing that Timber Line wouldn't dare. He's full of tricks, I tell you. He likes to do things that nobody else would ever think of. And he wins out, because most folks is fools like you, and he surprises 'em. That's his way . . . quick and mighty daring. That's why he ain't never been caught."

Still the girl was obdurate. "It ain't possible," she said. "This gent has a plumb honest eye. You can't fool me."

"Why? Are you Missus Solomon, maybe?"

"I know a crook, I tell you."

"Where'd you learn that?"

"I been raised among 'em," said the girl brutally.

The woman crimsoned with hatred. "When Uncle Tom hears this . . ."

"He won't believe you," said the girl, shrugging her shoulders. "He'll say you're just trying to make trouble for me."

"He . . ." Then the truth of this suggestion made its way home into the mind of the other, and she was choked with impotent fury, which is its most violent species.

"Besides," said the girl, "what'd Timber Line be coming here for?"

"You ask that? Why, he's come to murder Tom, that's why. And then he'll cut the throats of the rest of us, so's there won't be none left to tell what was done. That's his way."

Again Marie shook her head. "I know an honest man," she asserted.

"You talk like a fool, girl."

"I'm right, though."

"Wait till Tom comes . . ."

At the moment the door was thrown open, and the long-expected Tom appeared. He was a big man, as thick of neck and chest as his son Sam would be when the latter grew to his full stature and weight. In a word, he was a giant. His rough clothes, wet with rain and twisted with the wind, made him seem even larger. He wore beard and mustaches which, for the lack of a barber, were occasionally hacked into shape with a sheep shears — the beard being chopped off just beneath the chin, and the mustaches in a similar fashion severed at the ends close to the corner of the mouth. And the coarse hair, cropped after this barbarous fashion, stuck out like the bristles on an old brush, worn into ragged unevenness. He was a man of perhaps forty-five, which suggested that his wife was even younger. Yet she seemed ten years his elder in age; certainly she was his senior in evil.

He gave them not a word as he came in. His hat he thrust back on his head without taking it off, and a long, black lock of hair tumbled down across his forehead and over his eyes. He took his station in front of the stove, first jerking open the door to the firebox so that the heat might come at him more readily. Almost at once steam began to rise from him as the warmth penetrated into his soaked clothing.

The attitudes of the women underwent a change the moment he appeared, although he did not deign a glance at them. Marie hastily took up the mending which her two conversations had interrupted. Her aunt hovered about her husband with a sort of cringing solicitude. The great mastiff, that had lain in the darkest corner for some time, now crawled forward on his belly and lay at the feet of the master, wagging his tail hastily when the big man so much as glanced at him.

"I'll fix up a snack," suggested the wife, still with her anxious hands locked together.

He made no reply until she had gone to the cupboard and brought out half a dozen dishes to the table. Then he said curtly: "I've et."

She returned the food to the shelves without a word of protest. "There's been no luck, then, Tom?"

He said nothing, but, instead of answering, he pointed to a corner of the room. The wife hesitated a single instant, and Marie forestalled, knowing with swift intuition exactly what he wanted. She was up from her sewing in a flash and brought him the pipe. That was not all. From his hip pocket, without being bidden, she extracted the stained tobacco pouch. From this she filled the pipe, packing down the contents with an expert finger. She offered it to him, and, while he placed the stem between his broad, yellow teeth, she lighted a match and held it, moving it in a little circle above the bowl until the tobacco was a round, red coal.

Then, half enveloped with the smoke of his strong puffing, she moved back and resumed her seat and her sewing.

"Tom," said the wife gently, "I got news. Timber Line is here!"

Tom tamped his pipe and said nothing.

"It's him," said the wife. "It's Timber Line himself."

The big man deigned to speak at last. "You're a fool," he said.

CHAPTER
FIVE

"Marie Learns The Story"

In the heavy silence which followed this pronounce-ment, the door swung silently open, and the three turned startled faces toward it. It was only Sam, returning with his rifle tucked under his arm. There was audible a faint sigh of relief, and Sam, without a word, put up his gun and took a place in an obscure corner, as though conscious that it was not well to bring the eye of his father upon him. The latter now chose to develop the announcement he had made.

"The trap caught Timber Line," he said. "I come down the trail and seen that the ground was caved in. I lighted a match and looked. There was hoofprints along the trail. And who but Timber Line would ride that trail at night? Nobody around here has nerve enough to do it."

"We got a gent in the house right now that has nerve enough, Dad," said his son.

Tom frowned upon him. "You don't talk no sense, Sam," he remarked.

"He come right down the trail," said Sam. "His hoss is out in the barn. Says that his hoss smelled trouble and jumped a place in the trail . . . and her hind legs knocked the head of the trap in. He just managed to pull her up on the far side."

Denial was dark in the face of Tom, but, in the face of so much detailed testimony, he could not speak at once. He waited silently.

Finally he said: "What sort of a looking gent is he?"

"Tallish. About six one."

Tom started. "What sort of a looking face?"

"Kind of thin, with a big forehead."

"Timber Line!" breathed Tom.

It seemed impossible that he could really show fear, so big in body and resolution was he. But now his face turned a greasy gray, and he caught up the gun that he had put down on entering.

"It's not Timber Line," broke in Marie Rochambeau.

"Eh?" said Tom, catching at a new hope again.

"She's a fool," said the hag. "She ain't got any sense. I knowed that it was Timber Line the minute that I laid eyes on him."

"What you got in your head, Marie?" asked Tom, waving to his wife to keep silence.

"He talks clean talk," said Marie. "Talks like a book, pretty near."

"That's Timber Line," muttered Tom.

And his wife nodded triumphantly.

"I tell you," said Marie, "this gent is a tenderfoot, pretty near. I know!"

"How?"

"I seen the palms of his hands. They're soft as a baby's."

"Timber Line," groaned Tom. "That's him. He never done enough work to raise a callous. That's him!"

Marie, amazed, could only sit patiently and listen and wonder.

"Sam," said the father, "slide up that ladder and have a look if he's really in bed or up and prowling around."

Sam turned white. He eyed the black rectangle into which the head of the ladder disappeared as though it were the mouth of a cannon. But much as he feared, he dreaded his father even more. Slowly he stole to the foot of the ladder, taking up a revolver as he went, and slowly, slowly he climbed to the top. His head and shoulders finally disappeared into the thick darkness above. There he remained for a moment, and then he began to make his descent. He came back to them with the color returning gradually into his frightened face.

"He's in bed, right enough," he said. "I seen the lump of his body at the far end of the room under the blankets."

"Maybe he stuffed something under the blanket to make it look like a man was still sleepin' there?" suggested the father of the house anxiously.

"I seen the light glint on the white of his face from the window by him," said Sam.

There was another general breath of relief at these good tidings.

"I don't make out," put in Marie Rochambeau, who still apparently clung to her first idea, "how it could be Timber Line, if he's up there sound asleep."

"Why not?" asked Sam. "And talk soft . . . he might hear."

They drew together, whispering, a ghostly group.

"Would Timber Line come right down into your house and dare to go to sleep in a bed? He ain't that much of a fool."

"You don't know him," replied Tom. "There ain't no fear in Timber Line."

"There's got to be fear in everybody," insisted Marie.

"Not in him. He's got an idea that, when his time comes, he'll be bumped off, but not before. He's got an idea that, no matter what he does, he can't save himself when his time comes, and no matter what other folks do, they can't get him before that time comes along. He's set in that. Look at the crazy things he's gone and done before this."

"And who but Timber Line," said Sam, "would ride the trail at night? There ain't three gents in the valley that would ride the trail in the broad daylight, let alone in the dark, let alone with a storm blowing up the valley."

Still Marie persisted in hunting for a way out of the difficulty.

"Suppose," she said, "that he and his hoss just happened to come onto the trail. There wouldn't be nothing strange in it, then. It'd be too dark for him or his hoss to see how steep the cliff was, and how high. There's plenty of trails narrower'n that one. It's the cliff that makes gents lose their nerve."

"Hark at her," said the crone. "That's the way she's been talking all evening. She lost her head, when she seen Timber Line. She'll be follering along after him, if he gets away."

"I'd sooner see her dead," said Tom gravely. "But Timber Line ain't going to get shut of me this easy. They's going to be a dead man in this here house before the morning comes."

"Uncle Tom!" cried Marie.

"Shut up, you fool. He'll hear you. What d'you want?"

"If you kill him . . . what'll happen to you?"

"What could happen?"

"For murder? Uncle Tom, they'd hang you."

"For getting rid of Timber Line? You talk plumb crazy, Marie. They'd give me a medal. I know ten sheriffs that would ride a thousand miles to shake my hand. That's the kind that Timber Line is. He ain't a man. He's a devil . . . damn his heart."

"But why should Timber Line be coming down here to get at you? Why should you figure that he'd be coming after you now?"

"They's a good enough reason. They ain't no call why I shouldn't let you know. Look here."

From his inner coat pocket he drew forth an envelope much stained and ingrained with dirt, and this he handed to Marie.

"Read it out loud . . . but soft," he murmured. "I want Sam to hear. The wife knows what's in it already."

The crone shuddered in sign that she did, indeed, know what the letter held.

What Marie Rochambeau found in the letter was a straggling scrawl that wandered painfully across the sheet, each letter made with a manifest and painful care. It was like the forced and labored writing of a school child. Yet the document was pages long and must have required hours of struggle for its composition.

"'Dear Tom,'" she read in a hushed whisper, "'the devil is turned loose on us. Timber Line is turned loose on us. Timber Line knows the truth about what we done . . .'"

She broke off reading.

"What was it that you did, Uncle Tom?"

"It's an old yarn. You might as well know it. You know that Timber Line made me come into his gang. That was the time when he *kept* a gang. There was ten of us, altogether. Not one of us wanted to be with that devil. But we was afraid to say so, even to one another. We all figured that every other man in the crowd was with Timber Line because he wanted to be. And we was each of us afraid to talk to the other boys.

"But one day Jasper Matthews up and says something that made me figure that he had the same idea that I had. I told him right out just where I stood. Then he comes back and tells me that he hates working with a loafer wolf . . . never know when you'll get teeth sunk into your back.

"Him and me agreed that something had to be done. But it was a month before we figured out what it could be. Then we decided to let in the law on Timber Line. We figured it out fine . . . Timber Line used to come down to Sanderson's Hollow and build a pair of fires on the hill. That was a sign for us to come to that place two days later. Jas and me worked it out that, when we

198

got the signal the next time, we would send word in to the town.

"We saw the sheriff and got everything fixed. We told him we could let him in on the way to catch Timber Line and break up the gang. But we showed him that, if he wanted us to work for him, he'd have to play the game only our way. The idea was that, if Timber Line was able to get away and then was to find out who'd set the trap for him, nothing would keep him from following on and killing the gents that had double-crossed him.

"So we told the sheriff that it would have to be this way. When he got the word from us, he was to send out his men and throw a circle around the hollow. Then, when everybody had come into the trap, he was to close in the circle and capture them that was inside. But he was to swear that he'd turn everybody loose except Timber Line. The reason was that, if he kept all except me and Jas, Timber Line would know that we was the ones that had betrayed him. But if he turned us all loose, Timber Line wouldn't know who or what to suspect. That was the way we schemed it out, for we figured that, even if Timber Line was took, he'd be a hard man to keep in prison. He'd be apt to get out, and then he'd sure kill the gents that had turned him over to the law.

"That was the way it worked out. When we seen Timber Line's signal the next time, we sent in our word to the sheriff, and then we went to the meeting. It all went smooth. The sheriff had nigh a hundred men stowed away in the bush. He simply put a wall of men around us. We couldn't get away or fight a way through. And Timber Line set the example by throwing down his guns and putting up his hands and hollering out that he surrendered.

"The rest done the same, of course. And the sheriff lived right up to his promise. He turned the rest of us loose, and he went on into town. He collected his reward . . . and two days later Timber Line was free and out. He'd melted through the wall of the jail, you might say. He killed two men, got a hoss, and rode for it. He dropped three more while they was hunting him through the hills. Most usual he didn't kill unless he plumb had to. But this time he was crazy mad, and killed for the fun of killing.

"He got away, and every man in the gang figured that he'd be hunted down in turn. But Timber Line must of made up his mind that it was too much work. He couldn't hunt down ten men, one after another. Most of the ten scattered all over the range. But me, I stayed put, right here. Which might've made it look like I was innocent. But Timber Line never trusted one of the ten after that. He hated us all, as you know. Now, go on with the letter. What I've told you will clear up the things that Jas has to say."

He ended this tale of foul betrayal and deceit and cruel cowardice with a perfect calm, as though it had never entered his brain that the things he had done to Timber Line were worse than murder itself. His wife and his son seemed equally contented with his narration. Only Marie Rochambeau shuddered a little before she began to read again.

Timber Line found me the other night in my shack. He come like a ghost out of the night and stood up there in front of me. And I must have looked sick. I sure felt sick.

"I've come in for a chat," he says, and sits down by the stove as friendly as you please.

I figured that there was trouble in the air, but I tried to put a face on it. I offered him something to eat, but he says that he'd et just a while before and wasn't no ways hungry. That looked mighty black to me, him not eating. Because you know as well as I do that there never was a time when Timber Line wasn't near starved for hunger.

But I didn't say nothing. I went on mixing up some pone and talking to Timber Line about some of the things that I'd heard he'd done. I asked him about the bank robbery at Elkhead, and he out and talked about it.

He told me everything. Seems that there was a crooked clerk that Timber Line had fixed. The clerk arranged everything. He even got the combination for Timber Line, and that was how he made such a slick job of it.

When he got through talking, I up and tells him that I'm mighty glad he trusts me enough to tell me all the facts, like that.

"I got a reason to talk," says he, "you'll never do no gossiping about me after today."

And with that, he slips out his Colt and drops it on me. I shoves up my hands. There was nothing else for me to do.

"Put down your hands," says he, "and I'll put down my gun. We'll fight it out fair and square."

I wouldn't do it. I knowed that I had no chance ag'in' him.

"Well," says he, "we'll try another way. Because you're the skunk that double-crossed me at the hollow. I seen it in your face."

I swore that I didn't have nothing to do with it, but he kept at it. Said he'd make me talk. He tied me hand an' foot ag'in' the wall. Then he heated a ramrod in the stove till it was red hot. And he come up and shoved it into my arm.

"Now," says he, "will you talk?"

As soonas I could speak I told him that I couldn't stand it and that I'd I had to, Tom. It was too much for me to bear. And there he stood ready to give me more of the same medicine.

I had to tell him the whole thing. I couldn't think of no lies. I told him all about you and about me, and, when I got through, he grins at me, like the devil that he is.

"You've told the truth," says he. "I guessed part of it before, and now I know! Jas, have you got any last requests?"

I says to him: "You ain't going to murder me, Timber Line?"

He says to me: "It ain't murder, it's justice. I'll fix you now. Then I'll drift south and get the skunk, Tom!"

"Timber Line," says I, "is it square to kill me for what you've made me talk?"

"I ain't interested in small points," says he. "The main thing to get is the hounds that double-crossed me."

And he ups with his Colt and shoots me in the head.

You'll wonder how I happen to be writing this to you, then? I'll tell you.

He thought he'd killed me, because he went off and left me there, all tied up. But, by and by, along comes Slim Campbell, and looked in on me. He cuts me loose. There was a mark on my forehead where the bullet had hit.

He throws a bucket of water on me, not to bring me to, but to see where the bullet had gone, he told me later. Dog-gone me, if I didn't open my eyes and groan. He couldn't believe his eyes, he was that sure that I was a dead man.

But he bandaged me up as well as he could and throwed me into his rig and takes me to town. There the doc starts to work on me, and he finds out that the dog-gone bullet had slid up along and over my skull, and not even cracked the bone. Just sliced through the flesh and bruised me pretty bad. And that was yesterday. Today I'm finishing this letter to you. Watch sharp, Tom. Maybe it'll take that man-eater two weeks to ride south to you, working along by nights, the way he does. But he's sure to come, and, when he does, you'll need to be all done up in armor plate, if you expect not to die. Good luck, and heaven help you. From Jas.

CHAPTER
SIX

"The Flight of Tiny Stones"

It was all, indeed, more than clear, when this epistle had been read. And even Marie Rochambeau hesitated for an instant in her allegiance to the cause of the stranger. For it seemed very likely that a man who could attempt murder with such cruel deliberation as that which Timber Line had used in attacking Jas was truly capable of coming into the house of a man he intended to kill, going to sleep, awaiting the time when the victim returned, and then slaughter him.

For Timber Line was, as everyone admitted, less a man than a monster. She had been raised up to consider that grave figure as a sort of legendary monster who lurked high up among the mountains and descended, now and again, into the valley to strike like a thunderbolt, inescapably, and then withdraw again into the fastnesses where no horse, no man could pursue him. He was a creature of terror and mystery. He was a bloodless demon whom no tender kindness could ever move.

He drew his name from the sections of the mountains where he chose to dwell. He did not wander through the forested sections of the lower slopes where ordinary men lurked from the hand of the law. Instead, he chose to mount to the bald fastnesses high above the timberline, where the last of the glaciers still moved, and where there was little life, saving that of insects and of mountain sheep. In these regions the storm-clean rocks were too hard to keep the print of a trail even of shod hoofs, or, if they took the imprint for a time, a fall of snow was sure to blot it out eventually. If the region was bare of trees behind which he could lurk, it was forested with crags of stone which were perhaps an even better shelter. And if it were a lonely district, which others would have shunned like death, it was universally admitted that Timber Line detested and despised human society.

He needed no companionship. His companions were the memories of the evil deeds he had done. His friends were, indeed, his hatreds of others. It was said that he was as remorseless to women as to men, and, although there was no proof that he had ever been brutal with one of the weaker sex, it was generally believed that sex would be no shelter from his cruelty.

Such was the picture that formed in the mind of the girl at the very mention of the name of Timber Line. Such was the horror which she felt that the word poisoned all the kindness which she had felt for the stranger that night. She had fallen into a happy dream with the stranger as the center of it. But now the dream was vanished, and she was looking at bitterly clear facts.

No one, it seemed agreed, would have come down that trail except the terrible Timber Line. The proof was that Timber Line was known to have ridden that trail both night and day in former times when he haunted this southernly region. For he rode a horse with the footing of a mountain sheep, and he was himself without nerves; he could not be afraid.

What if the stranger were, indeed, this monster from the upper mountains?

"Now," said Tom, who had been gradually making up his mind, "we've come to the time when we got to do something. Sam, it'll be you and me that got to do the work. And it'll take the both of us. I go first. You come after me. How's your Colt?"

Sam, very white, but strangely steady, took out his gun and broke it open.

"Clean as a whistle," said the father approvingly. "The two of us ought to do the work . . . providing he don't wake up too soon."

The blood of Marie froze. Out of her horror was born the sudden certainty that the stranger was not and could not be Timber Line.

"You'll not murder him . . . in the middle of his sleep . . . like this?" she gasped out.

"Wait until he wakes up and murders us?" Uncle Tom asked calmly. "We ain't such fools as that, girl. You shut up. The two of you womenfolk get out of the house. This ain't no place for you. Never know what'll come up at a law trial. But things which you ain't seen and ain't heard are things that you don't know. That's the way that it works out in the law."

There was nothing to do but obey him. She thought, for a wild moment, of raising an outcry. But if the fellow were, indeed, Timber Line, what better did he deserve than the fate which was coming to him?

She left the house. The hag went in one direction; she herself ran around the house and stood under the window that was at the end of the attic and through which the starlight had fallen upon the face of the sleeper and shown it to Sam.

What was that window about to look in upon and witness now? And she saw, in her mind's eye, the two stealthy hunters crawling down the attic floor, moving upon hands and knees, and feeling cautiously for every step of the way. For a single sharp squeak of the floor would be enough to betray them, perhaps, and rouse the ear of the unconscious victim before them. Then, if it were Timber Line, he would be a match for them both, perhaps. Perhaps it would be a threefold slaughter by the dull light of that window.

She could not endure that waiting. The silence of the house was a mortal, deadly thing. Then she heard something stir in the room beneath. They had not yet mounted the ladder, then. No, perhaps they were still in close consultation, head to head, and planning every detail of the hideous crime which they were about to commit in partnership.

What a beginning in life was this for Sam? The brutal, cruel boy, as she well knew, had little that was good in him. But such work as this would give him the taste for blood that might never leave him. And, no matter how hideous the crimes of Timber Line might be, nothing he had done could justify this damnable night's work.

She waited no more to think over the points of the thing that had come into her mind. She leaned and scooped up a light handful of gravel that was scattered at her feet, and she threw the pebbles with a sure and strong hand. She heard them tinkle lightly against the glass of the windowpane — the only pane in the house that was still uncracked or unsmashed.

Then the flight of tiny stones whirred down and rattled faintly against the ground. She stepped back and waited. It was a night of divine beauty. The wind, which had changed and raged down the valley for a time, had lasted long enough from that direction to wash the sky clean of clouds. Then it had fallen away to whispers. Every star was out with a steady or a broken shimmering, and through the rain-washed, thin air of the mountains they burned down close above her head.

On the left the hills lifted up big and bold and then rolled away to the south like waves. To the right arose the strong face of the cliff that walled that side of the valley, an impenetrable fence. She eyed it narrowly, seeing everything with a strange clearness in spite of the tumult that was in her brain. And, far above, she saw the starlight glinting faintly along the narrow ledge that ran down the face of the cliff, doubling back here and there, and then continuing down to the foot.

That was the trail which the stranger had ridden on this night in the midst of utter darkness, with the terrible force of the storm prying at him. Indeed, it seemed to her that no one saving Timber Line himself could have followed such terrible footing safely to the valley below. Again, hard-hearted as she was, she almost regretted the warning which she had given to the sleeper in the attic above her. But, very likely, he had not heard the sound; it had melted into his dreams like the mild rattle of raindrops. At least, she would do it no more, and she threw down the second handful of the pebbles that she had scooped up.

Then, behind her, a shadow stirred, or a substance as softly moving as a shadow. She turned quickly around, her teeth set in fear and excitement, and she saw just behind her the outline of a man slipping up on her — the outline of a figure identical with that of the stranger.

Had he slipped out, then? It was just possible that a very active man, reckless of danger and strong of hand, might have opened the attic window, and so climbed down the almost sheer side of the house to the ground beneath. Yet, when she remembered the stranger she had fed that night, she could not believe that he was half athlete enough to have done such a deed. It did not seem possible.

She stared hard at him. She could make out a thin face, but no more.

"I'm sorry," said the stranger, "to disturb you . . . but I must ask you to make no noise. Do you understand? Not a whisper."

"Thank God," breathed Marie.

The other seemed a little taken aback. "For what?" he asked.

"It is not his voice."

"What are you talking about?"

"Nothing you'll understand. Who are you?"

"Come back with me behind that shed, out of sight of the house, and I'll tell you."

She shrank back, and the fear which was lying in the corners of her brain rushed all across it, numbing her faculties and making her faint.

"Come," he said, and stretched forth in the starlight a long and slender hand — bony, slender fingers, very like the hand of the man in the house. And yet different. There was a shadow not of night on the back of that hand. Now she shuddered in earnest. It was a hairy paw, like that of an ape.

She could not resist. The bright eyes which regarded her from beneath the steep shadow of the broad-brimmed hat fascinated her with terror. So she took a pace forward. Coming thus closer, she could make out the features of that thin face, cleanly carved, bony — a high, hawk nose, a long, lean jaw with a square end — a wedge-like face as cruel and cold as the face of a bird of prey. And then the truth came sharply home to her.

"Timber Line!" she breathed.

CHAPTER
SEVEN

"Because of a Bandanna"

Through all the trouble and danger which lived in the air about him on this night, Jerney slept with perfect calm. His very dreams were happy ones. He was out of all danger, even in his sleep, and beheld himself pacing to and fro in the garden of his suburban home and looking across the meadow to Madame, who lifted her proud head to answer his whistle. He was concluding that he would never be able to leave her behind him, whenever he went, when he left the great West again.

At this moment his eyes opened. He had heard something like the rattling of a burst of raindrops against the window-pane beside him, and so he closed his eyes and prepared for the sweeping of deep sleep over him.

Yet, as the wave of slumber began to pass over his brain, one disturbing thought remained on guard to fight it back. Although sleep strove hard to overwhelm him and washed out all but one spark of consciousness, that one spark of thought remained alive to say to him: *There was something odd in the sound of that shower of rain. In fact, it wasn't rain at all.*

What was it, then, that had sounded there with a sharp and metallic pattering against the glass? A shower of hail, of course, he told himself. But now the small debate had wakened him to such a point that both of his eyes were opened, and he was frowning drowsily into the darkness around him. His whole body and mind ached with the want of sleep. The fatigues of the day were only beginning to be soothed from his tired muscles.

It was rather odd, he now thought, that the hail had ceased almost as soon as it had begun — most strange that neither rain nor hail should be sounding upon the thin roof just a little above his head.

He turned in the blankets, and now, through the window and far away, he saw the small shining of a star — another and another. This was very queer, indeed, and the strangeness of it made him rouse from his sleep. For here was a perfectly clear sky, and yet, out of it, hail had fallen only the instant before.

Jerney pushed himself into a sitting posture, and, resting there upon his arms, he scowled into the thick blackness and tried to recall himself. Down the attic room he could see the distance to the next rafter, and that was all. Then, suddenly, he recalled the whole evening by steps and sections — the arrival, and how he had forced his entrance in spite of the unwillingness of Sam, and how he had been served by Marie Rochambeau, and how her pretty dark eyes had dwelt upon him, wistfully, sadly, happily at once.

He was wide awake now, thinking of her, and, indeed, he wondered that he could ever have slept.

From that window beside him the noise had come of the clicking against the windowpane. It now seemed to him that there might be some significance in it, so he slipped from the blankets and kneeled at the window to look out. There, just beneath him, stood the very lady of his dream — there was Marie Rochambeau herself with her head raised and her eyes fixed upon him.

She was not alone. A tall figure of a man was coming up behind her with a light, long stride. Marie turned upon him, and started as though in the greatest surprise. He watched them confer for a moment, until the long arm of the man went out and he held forth his hand as though summoning her. By what right should he do that?

By a right, at least, which she could not resist, for now he saw her take a step forward. She seemed to be looking most earnestly into the face of the tall man. Jerney would never forget that picture.

That was not all. They debated for a brief instant — about what he could not guess. Then the stranger raised his head. It was too dark for Jerney to see his features, but he was sure that his eyes were fixed upon the window in the attic behind which Jerney knelt. More than that, he could have sworn that the night prowler had looked past the glass of the window and actually recognized him.

That, however, could not have been the case. Satisfied by his glance around him that he was unobserved, he caught at Marie Rochambeau and gathered her suddenly in his arms. She was swept from the ground, her head covered, and her outcries stifled, and so in an instant the stranger had glided out of view around the corner of the nearest shed that stood behind the house.

Jerney did not pause. He was too horror-stricken to cry out. His vocal chords were paralyzed, but his body was not, and he moved to get down to her assistance as soon as he could. He whirled from the window, and he leaped down the long, low attic room like a sprinter coming out of his marks. He made two long strides, and then his shoulder passed into something soft and heavy. A body went down before him, and a curse which was half stifled for the lack of breath was panted in the ear of Jerney.

Just before him, a gun flashed almost in his eyes, but so hastily aimed that the bullet whirred past his ear. By that flash he had seen the frightened and contorted face of Sam in front of him. And he struck out with all of his might. There was no great strength in those thin arms of his, exercised more at pushing a pen than at any more muscle-building work, but his wild swing landed flush upon the gaping mouth of Sam, and the terror of the big fellow did the rest. He flopped heavily upon the floor of the attic. The next moment the heel of Jerney struck the stomach of the prostrate man, and then he was at the ladder into the kitchen below. He grasped the top rung and lowered himself below the floor just as another gun barked in the darkness, and another bullet combed past his head.

He flung himself clear of the ladder and crashed down to the floor. There was one well-smoked lantern burning in a corner of the room. It made the table and the stove and the clothes against the wall so many odd streaks of shadow, formless as clouds. The bars of the lantern sides checkered the floor oddly.

Jerney reached the door and cast it wide. Then he remembered in the nick of time that he was not armed. He thought of turning back for a gun. But what was a gun in his hands, saving a helpless and a harmless threat? He put the thought of the gun behind him and fled from the door, intent on doing what work he could with his bare hands.

For the men of the house would not be far behind him. He could hear the boots of someone strike the living room floor behind him even as he bolted from the open door into the night. And a second man was following down the ladder.

He raced straight in the direction of the point at which the stranger had disappeared, carrying Marie Rochambeau with him. He turned the corner of the shed and saw nothing before him. He darted down the length of the barn. Certainly the tall man, burdened with Marie as he was, could not hope to move with any great rapidity. Yet he had covered distance miraculously well so far.

And then, whirling around the end of the shed, he saw them in the distance, the form of the tall fellow swinging into the stirrups, and the girl cradled in his arm as though she had been no more substantial than a form in paper and sawdust.

He veered away in this new direction, running like a frightened deer, for he had not many seconds now if he wished to come at the rider before the latter were settled in the stirrups and rode away at the full speed of his spurred horse. So he shot past the end of the shed again, and, as he did so, two running forms came out of the night and crashed against him. He went down like a runner on the football field, tackled in mid-career. He went down solidly, and the back of his head struck against a stone with an almost metallic click. Then the light of thought went out, and he was asleep.

"He's coming to, fast enough," said a deep and heavy voice, and a voice which he recognized as that of Sam added: "Sure! You can't kill a skunk like him. Got nine lives!"

He was lying on the floor of the living room of the shack. What he first saw was the face of the crone of the place as she stood back at a little distance with her arms akimbo and a grin of the most profound malice upon her features. She could not have looked more like a caricature of a witch than she did at that instant. Beside him crouched the two men of the house, the father and the son, heavy shouldered, thick of hand.

"Clap a gag in his face before he starts yelling and brings Marie in to see what's happened! Where's Marie, anyway? She's mostly close around when there's any mischief happening!"

"She run like a scairt rabbit," said the woman in reply. "I seen her going for the trees like a whirlwind. She won't be back for more'n a spell."

In the meantime, Sam, with expert and brutal hands, made the gag for the victim, wadded it into his mouth, and tied a bandanna about his head.

"Sit him up," said the father of the house. "Slam him into that there chair, Sam."

Sam obeyed the very letter of the order. His stomach was still sore and aching where the hard heel of Jerney had landed in it. He heaved up the captive and crashed him down in a chair with such force that Jerney felt his senses spin again.

"Bring a light!" commanded Tom. "Dog-gone me, if I can see any more than a shadow of Timber Line."

Timber Line? mused Jerney to himself.

For he had heard, of course, of that strange and terrible robber whose depredations had so often filled the newspapers. Why that name should be used now and applied, apparently, to him, was more than he could possibly understand. But he guessed at some sort of a grim humor clumsily at work here, behind a screen.

"There ain't much weight to him," said Sam.

"There never was," answered the father.

"Didn't seem much strength, neither."

"Timber Line didn't have no chance. We hit him quick and by surprise . . . we didn't have no idea of what we was running into, until we landed on him. If it hadn't been for that, you'd've seen him working like a wildcat. We was lucky, and that's all, Sam . . . you can lay to that."

It *was* Timber Line, then, that he was mistaken for, Jerney understood. The very thought was too appalling. It chilled his blood and made him dizzy and sick. For what fate would come to him, if he were really identified with that arch-marauder?

"Bring the lantern over and let's have a look at him," said Tom. "Damn me, if it ain't sort of queer to have Timber Line lyin' helpless at my feet . . . him that nobody never got the better of before. Hurry up and bring the lantern over, Sam. I want to see what the last few years have done to him."

Sam brought the lantern. The light fell full upon the face of Jerney, and he waited impatiently for Tom to exclaim that they had caught the wrong man. But he did not exclaim at once; neither when he spoke was it to that effect. He only said finally: "Well, damn my eyes, if he don't seem to of growed young, instead of old. But they's some gents that way. They don't turn old till the end. Then they go with a snap."

To Jerney it was incredible and horrible beyond words. It could not be that he was mistaken for the celebrated desperado, and yet here was the evidence of his eyes and his ears to prove to him that he *was* so mistaken.

"What's the next thing, Dad?" asked Sam, who was apparently in an ecstasy of fear and delight.

"I dunno," said Tom. "We got to think this here all over. Hey, gimme my pipe."

The pipe was brought. He loaded and lighted it himself, and then sat down and looked Jerney in the face, never stirring his eyes from the gagged and bound man, whose legs and arms were securely lashed to the chair in which he sat by Sam. While he puffed at his pipe, he scowled in deep thought.

"There'll be a lot of talk, Dad," said Sam. "I reckon that, when we take this here gent into town, they're

218

going to stare, eh? And the reward, Dad! Dog-goned, if I didn't forget all about that!"

"You did? That proves that you're a fool, then, Sam. I guess that fifteen thousand dollars ain't to be forgot so soon or so easy. Fifteen thousand . . . dog-gone me, if it ain't a fortune, Sam. We could buy the farm down to Loggerhead with eight thousand and have seven thousand working for us in the bank."

Here he turned his head sharply around as he heard a moan. He observed his wife standing transfixed, with a smile of joy more than earthly upon her face as she contemplated all that fifteen thousand dollars would do for her.

"Shut up!" said her husband. "Shut up. I don't want to hear your yap, d'you see?"

She drew back into the corner of the room. But still her eyes were like fire as they dwelt on the face of the captive. And Jerney struggled to gain the use of his tongue. One word might convince them. Beyond a doubt, it was the masking bandanna that was tied across the lower part of his face which made Tom think him the outlaw. He looked on Jerney, convinced that the latter was Timber Line; and the bandanna made it impossible for him to distinguish most of the features that would have shown him at once this was a younger and altogether different man.

"Look here," said Sam. "He's trying hard to speak. When do we let his hands go?"

"Never, you blockhead!"

"Not even to take him to town?"

"Not even to take him to town. Sam, damn me, if you don't grow more of a fool everyday of your life. Sure his hands'll be free, when we take him into town, but he'll not care about that one way or the other."

CHAPTER
EIGHT

"Writing On The Floor"

That was the plan, then, Jerney saw. He was to be butchered before the coming of the morning light; then his body was to be taken to the town where the reward would be claimed for the capture and killing of Timber Line. For the reward was equally great for the apprehension of the criminal, dead or alive. And here he sat, with delivery for himself in the price of a single word. Nay, if he could only induce them to shift the bandanna from his face where it had been tied in the darkness before the lantern was brought, he would be kept from a dog's death.

That was not all. For what was becoming of Marie Rochambeau? As he thought of her, his own agonies became a mere nothing.

"You mean," said Sam, "you ain't going to take him in alive?"

"I mean that I got some sense," said Tom. "There he sits. There's the great Timber Line. Well, he's worth fifteen thousand dollars the minute that I'm sure of him. How can I be sure of him? By knocking the lights out of him. Long as he's living, he's dangerous. He's showed that a pile of times before. Three times they

221

caught him, and three times they had the irons on him, and three times he's gone clean away and got loose from the whole of 'em! He's walked right through a whole townful of folks. Suppose he was to get a chance to do some of his work on us, eh?"

Sam shivered. "You're mostly always right, Dad," he admitted. "But ain't we going to have a chance to hear him talk?"

"Why the devil should we?"

"He could tell about a whole flock of the things that he's done. Maybe he could clear up a lot of the mysteries that are hanging around the mountains. If he wanted to talk, it's said that he could set free a whole lot of them that are in prison doing time for the killings and the robberies that he pulled off by himself. We ought to give him a chance to do a little talking before he dies, Pa."

This suggestion was considered by Tom with a form of deliberation. He turned it back and forth through his mind with the greatest care, but apparently he could see no danger in it.

"So long's his hands and his feet are tied," he said, "I guess there ain't any trouble coming from him. Go ahead and take the gag out of his mouth, Sam. We'll have a little fun before the finish of him."

Sam stretched forth his hand to do what he was bidden, but he was stopped by a shrill cry that came from the lips of his mother.

"Sam, stop. Tom, are you plain crazy? You want to throw away fifteen thousand dollars? I tell you, if you do, if you let him talk, you'll never get a cent. More fools has been persuaded and talked into trouble than have been hurt by the hands of rascals like him. He's a talker. He could make anything seem real and right. That's him!"

Tom nodded at once, as though he saw the force of such a remark.

"Keep off from him, Sam," he directed. "Damned, if the old woman ain't got an idea. She only gets one a year, but, when it comes along, it's worth something. Keep off from him. Yep, she's right. I've heard of more trouble done by the persuading of gents than was ever done by the harming of 'em with the guns or hands. We'll let that tongue of his rest."

"The sheriff will sure take it hard, Dad."

"The sheriff be damned! I say that the time has come for us to finish this here game. We ain't going to sit here all night and look Timber Line in the face. Gimme your gun, Sam."

Sam reluctantly handed over the Colt.

"Look! Look!" cried Tom, starting from his chair in amazement. "Timber Line is losing his nerve!" He started back into the middle of the room. "Look how pale he's turned, Sam. Look at the perspiration on his forehead. Look at the way he shakes and wriggles in the chair."

"I see," said Sam. "But ain't it enough to make him wriggle about a little?"

His father turned upon him a glance of deepest scorn to repay such a lack of understanding.

"This ain't no common skunk," he said coldly. "This here is Timber Line! And if I was to tell the world that

Timber Line lost his nerve before he died, the rest of the world would up and tell me that I was a liar."

He turned upon his wife. "Gimme some whiskey. I need it bad. Timber Line busting down. That ain't possible! If he goes this way, how'll the rest of us go? What'll happen to me, when I come to the end of my rope . . . ?"

"Why, Dad, nothin'll ever happen to you. You'll pass out in a bed, quiet and comfortable. And part of them fifteen thousand dollars will pay for the bed that you lie in."

But his father only favored Sam with a sour look, and reached for the heavy jug that his wife dragged toward him. It was a five-gallon jug of the heaviest, thickest earthenware, and since it was full, or nearly so, there was close to forty pounds of liquor in it. Yet such was the might and the muscular cunning of Tom that he raised the jug, tipped it over the bend of his right arm, and poured down his throat a long portion of moonshine whiskey. He lowered the jug again, shook his head as the fiery stuff burned its way home in him, and then lowered the jug to the floor.

"They's a need of whiskey now and then," he said, wiping his mouth with the back of his hand. But he added savagely: "Keep off from that jug, Sam. You ain't old enough to handle that sort of stuff. Keep off from it!"

Sam snarled at the forbidden fruit and showed his father his yellow teeth behind a curling upper lip. Yet he dared not disobey. He stepped back, looking from the whiskey jug to the captive.

"If he's yaller," he said to his father, "too bad that we should waste any time with him. Let's finish him off!"

He handed to his father the gun for which he had been asked before.

Here, however, the wife put in again, saying: "Get out of here with him, Tom. I ain't going to have my floor all messed up. That sort of a stain don't come out, and you know that it don't work out of wood. Take him outside, and I don't care what you do with him, but I ain't going to have my kitchen spoiled!"

Tom hesitated, glowering at her, as though he much preferred to do his foul work in comfort, rather than take his victim into the obscurity of the night where he might need two shots, perhaps.

However, there was something unanswerable in the last remark of his wife, and he sullenly prepared to obey her.

"Cut his legs loose," he said to Sam, "and then tie his hands behind his back . . . tie his hands first . . . that's the way. They ain't no danger. I'm right here with the gun, and, if he tries a wrong move, I'll blow his head off. Just the way he would've blowed the head off of Jas."

Sam, accordingly, freed the hands of Jerney, one by one, and secured them with invincible strength behind his back. When this work was done, he leaned and slashed through the ropes that bound the legs of the captive with a single stroke of his long and keen-bladed hunting knife.

"Look here," said the father, "there ain't any call to spoil so much good rope as that. But it's done now.

Besides, I guess that we're going to get enough money out of him, so's we can afford to have a new rope wasted on him."

Such was his complacence that he actually chuckled. There was a moment of pause before Jerney was dragged from his chair. Once raised from it, he was no better than a dead man, he knew. In that brief interval, while Sam was joining in the grim laughter of his father, Jerney scratched letters hastily upon the floor. There was a rough-headed nail projecting a little from the heel of his boot. With that nail he inscribed the letters, drawing them in roughly — drawing them in by the feel alone, unable to look down at the word he was trying to make.

Then Sam jerked him to his feet as the father rose.

"Hey, wait!" cried the crone, now coming forward again, for her beady little eyes had missed nothing. "He's been trying to write on the floor . . . he's made some letters . . . what are they, Sam?"

"The devil he has? Look here! Dog-gone me, he has. Here's what the letters are . . . M-a-r-i . . ."

"Marie!" cried Tom. "What the devil has he to say about her?"

"Shall I take the gag out of his mouth?"

Tom hesitated. "Nope . . . I ain't going to listen to his lies."

"Let him write on the floor another word, then."

Sam thrust the prisoner into the chair once more.

Now that Jerney could lean forward a little and look down at the writing that he was inscribing upon the kitchen floor, he worked with far greater speed and

226

surety. After the word — Marie — he promptly scratched: Gone.

"Marie gone?" echoed Tom.

"He's talking fool talk," said the crone. "Let her go. He don't know nothing. Marie is safe. There ain't nothing could bother a wild thing like her, I guess."

"Maybe not and maybe yes," growled the big man of the house. "I dunno . . . where did she go?"

The nail in the heel of Jerney promptly scratched upon the floor: "Timber Line."

"What sort of talk? Timber Line?" roared Tom.

"He's makin' fools of you all," said the crone.

"There's something in this. Damned, if there ain't something wrong in it."

And, placing his large and powerful hand upon the bandanna that was wrapped around the lower part of the face of Jerney, he wrenched at the cloth with such power that he rent it easily in two.

As Jerney spat out the gag from between his aching jaws, and as Tom cast the torn bandanna away, the latter cried out aloud in his voice of thunder: "In the name of heaven, this ain't Timber Line . . . this is his kid brother, maybe, but this ain't Timber Line!"

There was consternation in the room. Both the men turned savagely upon the crone.

"You've seen Timber Line," said Tom. "And you'd ought to've knowed his face. It was you that sent us off on a wrong trail. And, by the heavens, you come nigh to being the death of a gent here that's plumb innocent of being what you thought."

227

He and his son turned upon Jerney with curiosity, and with some shame.

"Fifteen thousand?" growlingly muttered Tom, as Jerney coughed and gasped to get back his lost breath. "We'd've been more like to have had our neck stretched with rope for the taking and the killing of this gent. Partner, I'm mighty sorry for what's happened. What's your name?"

Here, however, as Sam freed his hands, Jerney arose and cried to them: "No matter about me, but for heaven's sake, do something about the girl!"

"Eh?" grunted Sam.

But Tom turned white. "What's come of Marie?" he asked sharply.

"Taken away by a fellow who might have been a ringer for me, and, therefore, I presume that he was Timber Line."

"Taken away?"

"I tell you what I saw! He's riding down the valley with her now!"

CHAPTER
NINE

"Pursuit"

He was astonished that brutes such as he had taken both father and son to be could show such emotion as they now exhibited. They showered him with questions. They learned how he had looked out from the window of the attic and had seen a tall, slender man wearing a wide sombrero — a man with a lean face, a light step, a strangely imposing bearing, come upon Marie Rochambeau and bear her away into the night. While they listened to this narrative, both father and son turned pale with rage and grief. Only the hag was not moved. She glowered upon the narrator of the odd incident, and not a gleam of sympathy appeared in her fierce eyes.

Then they started into action. They snatched up a lantern, and they fled together to the barn. Here the horses were roused from sleep, brought lurching to their feet, and saddled in all haste. Fast although the other pair was, they were no sooner in the saddle than Jerney was at their heels, holding Madame upon a tight rein. She, most enduring and tough of mustangs, was already in fine fettle for a run. She shook the sleep out of her head, and then began to dance. The other two animals seemed strong and full of running. It no longer seemed to Jerney a hopeless gap of time since Timber Line had swept his victim away. He began to hope, and with hope came a sudden conviction that, before this hunt was over, Marie Rochambeau would be recovered to safety, Timber line would be punished, and the sun of the next day would bring them all happiness.

Sam rode first, swinging a lantern in his right hand and reining his mustang with his left. He kept the flame of the lantern turned so low that even a storm of wind could hardly have blown it out, and, when he came to a place where he was in doubt as to the direction in which the trail led, he paused, turned up the flame in the lantern, and thus leaned far to the side and brought both his eyes and the light close to the ground. In this manner he made up his mind in a minute exactly what he wished to know.

In fact, Sam took command of the situation. His father and Jerney fell well to the rear, and Sam directed operations with his light in the lead. The elder man took the occasion of the first halt to lay his hand kindly on the shoulder of Jerney.

"I take it right kind of you to give us a hand tonight," he said. "There ain't been any call to stand in with us the way you're doing ... nothin' but bad treatment ..."

"Forget that," urged Jerney. "If she's brought back safe from that demon, I'll give you my word that I'll never think of the rest. Do you think there's a chance that we ... ?"

230

"If it was anybody else but Timber Line," said the father gravely, "I'd sure say that we had better'n a chance . . . I'd say that we was sure to run him down. Because nobody can get shut of a trailer like Sam. He's got a nose like a bloodhound, you might say. He sort of smells and guesses his way along a trail. It ain't a question of him finding the trail . . . it's only a question of our hosses being able to ride fast enough to catch up with Timber Line."

"And his horse is carrying two," said Jerney enthusiastically.

"His hoss is carryin' two right now, maybe," said Tom gravely. "But will he be carryin' two, when we start in to press him?"

"You mean?"

"They's nothin' beyond Timber Line. He's done so many murders that life and death don't mean nothin' to him. He ain't like a man, I'd say. There . . . by the heavens, even Sam is stuck."

The proceedings of Sam had been to the eye of Jerney most remarkable. For his own part, as he rode out under the wide, dim sky of the night, and looked about him on the wilderness of trees and of rocks which choked the valley, it seemed to him the most utter madness to continue on the trail by night. But Sam went at his work as though there were not a million hiding places in which the fugitive could hide both himself and his captive.

First of all, he had gone to the site at which Jerney had with his own eyes observed the outlaw mounting his horse with the limp form of the girl in his arm.

There he cast around him, swinging the lantern in a swift circle before his glance took up what it wanted. Then he made his horse leap forward, at the same time turning down the flame of the lantern to a mere dull eye of light. He rode straight on, with a perfect confidence, winding through the trees and swinging along among the rocks as though he had the sun shining strongly to tell him the way that the flying horseman had gone.

It was a quarter of a mile, indeed, before he made a halt in his gallop. And this was hardly a halt. He brought his animal out of the gallop to a sliding stop at the head of a strong and high point of land that stepped out from the trees and looked out over the river. Here he swung his lantern down to the ground, but the very first glimpse seemed to tell him all that he desired to know, for he promptly reined his animal around, swung to the right, and rode on straight up the valley at the full speed of the mustang.

What he could have made out in such a glimpse at the ground was more than Jerney could imagine. But he acted, thereafter, as though he had read a set of directions carefully prescribing the course that Timber Line and his horse had taken.

They reached a steep slope up which the horses had to walk, and on the way Jerney was free in the expression of his wonder of the fashion in which Sam held a trail.

"It looks sort of mysterious," admitted the father. "Partly it's because Sam knows every trail along the valley, though. And partly it's because he uses common

232

sense. But most, I guess, it's because he's got a sort of a instinct for the trail. You'd think that he was a hound, working out a puzzle. Look there, now!"

For, as they reached the top of the rise of ground, they found themselves among a nest of rocks. Those hard surfaces would have smothered a dozen trails, even those made by the hard hoofs of horses. And, to complicate the problem, on the farther side of the rocks there were a full half dozen possibilities which the fugitive rider might have taken for his descent, and each would have brought him into the upper valley of the river by a highly different route.

Sam, in the meantime, had thrown himself quite out of the saddle, turned up the flame of his lantern to the verge of smoking, and now he was running back and forth among the rocks, bent almost double. Once he hesitated, once he paused and dropped upon his knees. Then he flung himself furiously into the saddle again and drove straight down the slope and into a thicket of trees, and led them on at so hot and sure a pace that twice they had to halloo to him to wait for them, and twice he directed them with his own answering shouts and then pushed valiantly ahead and let them come on after him as well as they could.

"Suppose he rides too far ahead of us?" asked Jerney finally, as they worked their horses side by side across a pleasant opening of the woods. "Suppose that he gets so far ahead that Timber Line sees him coming alone . . . ?"

"I dunno what would happen," said Tom dubiously.

"But you say Timber Line . . . ?"

"He's a man-eater. But so's Sam, when he gets on a trail. He's got the instinct, I tell you."

It half sickened Jerney to hear of it, and yet he was fascinated.

"I've been north and seen a little red-eyed ferret come snaking it along a trail so dog-gone hot for blood that he'd run right across my boots and pay no more attention to me than if I'd been a dog-gone tree. That's the way with Sam. When he gets on a trail, he's plumb wild, and don't see nothin' nor hear nothin', except the thing that he's huntin'!"

Not once, in fact, as they worked through the night, did young Sam turn back to call a cheerful word to those who were following according to his guidance.

"In the old days," said the proud father, "when they was Indian troubles, I guess maybe he would've been a pretty mean, man-sized scout, eh?"

The morning was coming now. It showed gray outlines of the mountains against the sky, at first. Then it brightened and gleamed on the waters in the gorge or trickled silver along the sides. It glinted here and there among the trees. And finally small things began to grow clear, and at last Jerney could see the color of the bandanna that their leader wore around his throat. It was a rich blue, dotted with white, and with a broad border of the most piercing blood-red.

With his back turned in this fashion and riding so straight in the saddle, with squared shoulders, the boy looked like an old and expert mountaineer, and Jerney could have smiled to himself to think how easily the

234

eyes will trick the mind into believing even what it knows is not so.

Morning showed not their guide alone. Presently a harsh and half-strangled shout came from the lips of big Sam. He pointed above and ahead of him and, at the same time, turned his face toward the two men behind him. Jerney saw a white, strained face, the mouth compressed, the eyes starting. He looked like one who had been hypnotized.

Far above them, in the direction in which he pointed up the side of the gulch through which they were riding, there appeared the wished-for form of Timber Line, riding his shining bay horse, and in front of him appeared a figure in yellow and blue.

Yellow and blue had been the ragged dress and cloak of Marie Rochambeau. And the heart of Jerney stood in his throat and half choked him. A cry similar to that of the son now broke from the lips of the father.

But at this the son turned abruptly in his saddle and grinned upon his father without mirth in his smile.

"Look here," he said, "I got some work to do . . . with a ghost." Now he laughed, indeed, in a crazy, high-pitched key at which Jerney marveled.

They were straining forward, working every muscle and every nerve to get at the fugitive.

"What's the matter with Sam?" asked Jerney, when he gained the next opportunity to speak with the father.

"It's Marie," said Tom reluctantly. "I knowed that it was coming at him all these weeks. But now I see the whole dog-gone thing. He's crazy about Marie

Rochambeau . . . plumb crazy, partner. And that's why he's acting this way on the trail."

Timber Line, of course, had disappeared long before in a winding of the trail above them. Sam left the trail and struck up a short cut on the face of the mountain, walking at the head of his horse, encouraging that wary animal, and helping it from place to place. The father hesitated, shook his head, and then ventured upon the same ascent. After them came Jerney. But it was nothing for Madame. The mustangs who traveled before her barely made it, but she floated over the difficulties as though they were not there, and Jerney verily believed that she could have gone up the sheer face of that cliff with her rider in the saddle.

They had gained greatly upon Timber Line by this maneuver. For now they saw him as they scrambled onto the upper trail and pressed forward again. They saw him so close that he shouted with astonishment, and Jerney caught a glimpse of a dark, ominous face, with solemn eyes and high cheek bones. He certainly was of more than a passing resemblance to Jerney. Yet there was a savage difference.

He was certainly startled by this sudden appearance of his enemies upon his rear. And touching his bay with the spurs, that splendid animal, in spite of the exertions of carrying double on a difficult trail for so many miles, was now able to spring into a swift gallop.

Tom, in the rear, moaned and swayed about in the saddle from side to side. And as they rounded the next corner of the rock, the hat was suddenly jerked off the head of Sam, very much as if he had turned into the

236

face of a strong wind blowing down the valley. A fraction of a second later, however, the report of the rifle rang about their heads. Sam had jerked his mustang in against the shoulder of the rock. And for a moment, he waited there, cowering. But suddenly he uttered a strange cry. It reminded Jerney of the wail of a beast — a beast he had never heard on the trail. Around the corner, where the rifle bullet had flown, sped Sam, with the cry still on his lips, and his long hair blown wildly behind his head. He had passed into a state of furious ecstasy. The rifle barked again in front of them, but Sam replied to it with a shrill yell of scorn. He had not been harmed.

"By the heavens!" gasped out Tom. "Timber Line has missed! And that's something that nobody has ever seen him do before. Timber Line has missed! When I heard his gun, I made right certain that my poor Sammy was dead."

With a yell of exultation on his own lips, he followed Sam around the corner of the cliff and rode recklessly along the trail that extended just before them.

At that moment, Timber Line appeared upon the point of the cliff just beyond. The momentary wavering of Sam had been taken such advantage of that he was now a considerable distance ahead. But, looking back, Timber Line apparently realized that his horse was far fagged, and that his enemy was better mounted and riding in more determined fashion than he had expected. At any rate, he did not hesitate in taking his next step. He cast suddenly from him the burden of the figure before him on the saddle.

Down flashed the yellow and the blue. It disappeared behind the corner of the rocks. It appeared again, farther down, falling headlong toward the river. And by the river it struck, and lay still among the rocks.

There was a scream of indescribable fury from Sam, a hoarse shout from Tom, and they both rushed ahead as fast as their horses could carry them.

CHAPTER
TEN

"The Heart of Timber Line"

Timber Line was not then the great object in the eye of Jerney. That spot of color far beneath him by the river's edge was what he must see. There was no hope, of course. Life would have been dashed out in a fall of a tithe of that distance. Yet, an uncontrollable impulse drove him on toward the horror. That brief glimpse of her the evening before was a thing that he could never forget, and now he sent Madame over the dizzy verge of the trail and plunged her straight down toward the blue and yellow shape beneath him.

It was like a swoop upon wings rather than a ride, that dip through the early morning light, down to the shadows by the waterside. For Madame, having once started her career downward, could not stop it. She was shooting along at great speed, and there was no ledge or slope great enough for her to come to a halt upon. She was carried on like a feather in the wind, and all that she could do, after her wild master had started her down the incline, was to break the force of the fall as well as she could by basing her hoofs for an instant, here and there, against the rocks which were

239

before her. Once she stuck her hoofs into a slide of gravel and stiffened her legs.

That was halfway down to the river, and she was going at a tremendous clip; a little more and the rate of progress would have been uncontrollable altogether and would have meant a certain death both for herself and for the rider. Even as it was, she started half a ton of gravel shooting for the river beneath her hoofs, but she herself was arrested in her rocket-like course.

She struck at the remaining rocks beneath her as a mountain sheep will do, bounding like a rubber ball from small projections, and so going easily down the most dangerous of cliffs in safety. To the amazement of Jerney, who had felt death take him by the throat half a dozen times in the descent, they stood suddenly upon the margin of the noisy little river, listened to the crowding echoes which came back hammer-like against their ears, and then he nerved himself and approached the fallen form.

Jerney dismounted from the back of Madame. He removed his hat, and, approaching without daring to fix his eyes upon death, he finally sank upon his knees and — before him he saw the branch of a tree wrapped in the cloak that Marie Rochambeau had worn.

He could not believe or understand. Then he saw that it had been simply a hideous farce. The outlaw had loosed the girl almost at once, no matter what had been in his mind when he first seized her. And, taking along her mantle, he had played this horrible joke upon Sam and Tom and Jerney.

240

Sick with relief, ready to weep with weakness and with joy, Jerney sat down upon a rock and took his head between his hands.

He looked up, hearing a cry nearby him, and there he saw the girl herself, waving and laughing to him across the river. To his amazement, she came to him at once, making nothing of the white swirling of the water, which had force, had she fallen, to take her in hand like a javelin and shoot her down its course. But she neither slipped nor fell, but sprang with perfect surety from the surface of one rock to the surface of another, until she came lightly to the shore on which he now stood up, and made his eyes glad with the sight of her.

The thing that had happened made them better friends than the passage of ten years of intimacy could have done. It enabled him to take one of her hands and listen while she told the tale. Timber Line had swept her away into the night, and she had been seized with such a horror, at the first, that she had fainted, as Jerney had thought when he first had seen her in the arms of Timber Line.

She had recovered almost at once, however, and found that, although he might be a very lion among men, he could be a lamb among women. He had halted his horse and explained to her calmly and gently that he had no wish to harm her; that he had returned into that country to revenge upon her father a terrible crime which the latter had committed at his expense and which had nearly thrown him into the hands of the law. But he had changed his mind, when he came close to the scene of action. He had sated himself with

241

bloodshed, he told the girl frankly, and now he would simply victimize Tom with a practical jest, although a terrible one. That shock would be the only repayment he would demand from her foster father.

She had consented to go freely with him as far as he might desire.

He had traveled on with her until near the morning, when he had discovered the close pursuit, and had decided that it would be too great a risk to climb the side of the cañon with his bay carrying double. So he had bidden her to get down, begged most politely for her mantle only and, in this fashion equipped, had broken off a bit of a rotten branch, draped the light branch with it, and so made off at a gallop across the ford of the river.

For her part, as it was then beginning to show a bit of the morning light, she had made out the pursuit and the pursued going up the wall of the ravine, climbing slowly along the height, and she had discovered that she could easily take a path along the riverbank and keep the whole little drama under her eyes.

So it was that she had seen the mantle and the branch cast down.

"For a minute," she said, "it looked so dog-gone like me falling, that I was almost afraid for myself. And then I saw you come shooting over the edge of the trail."

She stopped, and drew in a great breath. "What a terrible thing to do!" she cried at him.

"Did you care, Marie?"

"Hush," she said. "We must find out what has happened on the trail, and let's pray that Timber Line got away . . ."

But, although she talked of Timber Line, he could tell by her flush that she was thinking of Jerney only. He knew, indeed, with such a perfect certainty all that was going on in her mind, that all his anxiety vanished. And he looked upon her almost with a sad seriousness. It might be many a day before she would listen to a thing that he must say to her, but, when he spoke, he knew what her answer would be. They would go East together.

In the meantime, what was happening up the trail?

"He's gone by this time," she said with much confidence. "He's played his joke, and now he's gone from them. He's such a man that they could never catch him."

But Jerney, remembering that wild cry from the boy as he had spurred along the trail, doubted. He left Marie Rochambeau with the command to wait there for him until he returned, and then he started for the trail alone.

He sent Madame up an unmarked trail to the height, winding back and forth. He went on foot, and she followed like a dog at his heels, snorting and shaking her head at the work, but never faltering. Although there were places which he could barely scale with clinging hands and feet, yet she was just behind him, when he reached the upper trail again. Then he threw himself into the saddle and galloped ahead.

243

He covered four full miles before he found the place. When he reached it, all was silence.

Three horses stood riderless in a nest of rocks, picking idly at blades of grass where they projected here and there from meager patches of moss or dirt. And in the center of the circle lay Timber Line, stretched upon his back with his eyes wide open and staring up at the morning sun. His smile was a thing that Jerney could never forget.

Near him was another. It was Sam, lying dead in the arms of his father, who sat cross-legged upon the ground, pleading with his son to look at him and speak to him. But Sam would never speak again.

The prophets had all been wrong. Timber Line had reached his end not at the hands of a posse of fighters, but a single man had ended him, and he had killed his slayer. So the story of the great outlaw ended.

They buried them both, afterward, among the same rocks which had seen them die. They buried them side by side, and Tom brought up a chisel and a hammer and hacked a brief inscription which told how that battle was fought, all in the mortal space of half a second.

As for Tom himself, he never carried to the town a claim for the money of the reward.